GREGORY NORMINTON

THE DEVIL'S HIGHWAY

4th ESTATE • *London*

4th Estate
An imprint of HarperCollins*Publishers*
1 London Bridge Street
London SE1 9GF
www.4thEstate.co.uk

First published in Great Britain by 4th Estate in 2018
1

A catalogue record for this book is
available from the British Library

ISBN 978-0-00-824375-3 (Hardback)
ISBN 978-0-00-824376-0 (Trade paperback)

Map and Hare, wood ant and bee-eater
drawings by John Walker

Printed and bound in Great Britain by
CPI Group (UK) Ltd, Croydon, CR0 4YY

MIX
Paper from
responsible sources
FSC C007454

In memory of my mother,
Catherine Norminton-Mallein
(1946–2015)

Those that despise Scotland, and the north part of England, for being full of vast and barren land, may take a view of this part of Surrey, and look upon it as a foil to the beauty of the rest of England; ... here is a vast tract of land, some of it within seventeen or eighteen miles of the capital city, which is not only poor, but even quite sterile, given up to barrenness, horrid and frightful to look on, not only good for little but good for nothing ...

DANIEL DEFOE, *A Tour Through the Whole Island of Great Britain*

It is not a celebrated patch of Earth. There are few books and no ballads about it. It is four thousand acres of plantation pine, grassland and heath, hemmed in by roads and houses and industrial estates. In autumn the air smells of mushrooms, in summer of resin and the slough of pine needles. There is a Roman road and an Iron Age hill fort. Few locals visit either, for our lives are too hectic: we drive everywhere and rarely walk. Yet set out on foot, at dawn, and you can sense the ancient place beyond the pines. Open to the sky. Fully itself perhaps only when experienced. Made by the eye that sees it.

RICHARD BOROWSKI, *The Blasted Heath*

The Roman road; the eagle's flight ... the meeting of present, past and future.

VALERY LARBAUD

BERKSHIRE

The

Bracknell
BRAG NELL o

Caesar's Camp
Hillfort
OLD FORT

The Devil's Highway

CALLEVA
ATREBATVM

o Finchampstead
FANSTED RICHES

o Crowthorne
CROWSTORM

HAMPSHIRE

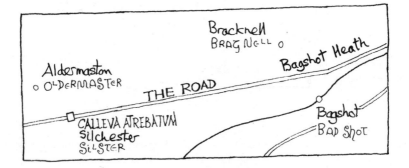

Bracknell
BRAG NELL o

Bagshot Heath

Aldermaston
o OLDERMASTER

THE ROAD

CALLEVA ATREBATVM
Silchester
SILSTER

Bagshot
BAD SHOT

N
W — E
S

ʰEAVE

Davys Way

The Thirsty

A30

Bagshot
Bad Shot

Windle Brook

Windlesham
Winsham

The Poors
Allotment

Deem
te

M3

The Winnel

The Empty

Pirbright
Ranges

miles
0   5

km
0   5

SURREY

1

Blueface

They worked in the byre by torchlight. In the stalls the cow bellowed. Andagin feared she would wake their father, who had succumbed to sleep like a warrior to his wounds.

'I looked for it,' he said, 'where I left it on the heath.'

'You mistook the place.'

'No.'

'The wind carried it off.'

'My cord was strong. She unfastened it. That means spring will come.'

'Spring always comes.' Judoc buried his fork in straw and dung. 'Corn dolls are for children.'

'But Ma says –'

'Ma says.' Judoc's voice was fierce but he took care to whisper: 'Will you stay her whelp for ever or would you become a man?'

Andagin felt the heat rise in his face. 'Do not call me whelp.'

'Why not? You whine like one. We need strong gods. Male gods like Taran. Thunder, not Earth. There – enough shovelling for me.'

They contemplated the steaming baskets. Judoc's face was hard to read for the torch burning behind it.

'Forgive me,' he said, 'for barking at you. But dreams will not save us.' He pulled Andagin into his arms and held him. He reeked of sweat and damp wool. 'Be strong,' said Judoc, and releasing Andagin he hoisted a basket to his midriff. Then he was gone.

Andagin patted the cow's hot flank. Taking the torch, he left the byre and walked into a weeping wind.

Snowflakes clung like burrs to his cloak and the stung tips of his eyelids. Winter searched for every rent in his gear. After the smoke and fug of the hut, after his father's nightlong coughing, the cold was welcome, a familiar enemy. Andagin contemplated the shuddering pelt of the heath. He pissed into the heather, expectorated as Judoc had taught him – a lusty hoick into the wind. He returned to the sorrow of the hut.

His mother was up and doing. He ducked out from under her tousling hand and sat beside the fire, where Nyfain greeted him with her habitual scowl.

'Where's your brother gone? Back to his pack again?'

Andagin shrugged. To think about last night's shouting made his heart clench. He watched Nyfain's fingers weave a basket of heather stems.

'Will you patch my cap for me?'

'Why would I do that?'

'It has a hole.'

'You made the hole.'

She was angry because Judoc was missing. Were he near she would have been no happier.

'The snow will get in.'

His cousin huffed and pulled the cap off his head. She inspected it and pushed a little finger through the gap. He watched her reach for the bone needle she kept and some thread.

'Will you be wheedling all morning or have you things to do? Now that your brother's at the hole game with his idiot friends.'

'There's no playing in winter.'

'Men are always at play.'

His mother reached down a bundle of mugwort from the rafters and tossed it into the fire. The medicinal fumes filled the hut and Nyfain's scowl tightened, for she hated the smell, though she knew better than to complain of it.

'You will be trapping again,' his mother said as she handed Andagin the pot of gruel.

When he had eaten his share and a mouthful of heather honey, he crawled to the bench and felt under it for his shoulder pack. His fingers found the arrows he stowed there: antler tips that Judoc had carved for him, back in the summer, before the strangeness took him.

'Vala. *Vala.*'

'Hush.'

'He's out again.' The coughing was long and liquid. 'Those hotheads ...'

'Drink this and lie quiet.'

Andagin took up his bow. He looked to where his father lay, hoping for a glance, a raised hand – some gesture that still had blood in it.

He left the hut disappointed.

To the east the cloud was stained with light. He bathed his gaze in it as he shrugged the pack more comfortably onto his shoulders. He sorted mentally through the contents. The knife was there. Some water in a gourd. Cordage. Her stone. He sensed, as if it were an old dog watching him, the hill fort at his back. He did not have to look at the smoking thatch and dilapidated fencing; he knew the talismans hooked on what had been battlements, wooden heads to keep evil spirits at bay. Andagin had rarely entered the fort. He knew only the cattle enclosure where livestock and brides were bartered, and the open field hedged with gorse where the dead were returned to the sky. There was also, forbidden to him and to all males, the shrine where his mother went to give him life, where Judoc was born and two others that never drew breath.

He thought about the dead babies. He could picture them only as dolls for an offering. 'She took them back,' his mother said. 'You must not be angry. She can take, for without Her we would have nothing to give.'

Andagin recited the story. He did it so that the dead might lie easy.

Long ago, when the world was young, there was nothing but forest from sea to sea. The sea was blue and the land was green, a sea of leaf and wood. There were many wolves and bears in the forest and men were their prey – for men could not find their way in the shadows and they never saw the face of the sun. One day our Mother took pity on men and sent a great wind to open up the forest. In the clearings made by fallen trees, corn and barley grew and heather for cattle to browse – and into these places men stumbled, giving thanks to she who had lifted the darkness. So to this day we worship our Mother for her mercy, and leave her corn dolls and a knot from the first sheaf. And we tread lightly on her mantle, for she is our parent that loves us, and will return us to life when our lives come to an end.

The hill fort burrowed out of sight. Andagin tracked south through croplands, praying to the hare that might sacrifice itself, to the woodcock and the fox. His belly was full only of hunger. He was sick of cutting the pith and seed from rosehips, of watery soup and stale hazelnuts.

Deep heather gathered like a rampart. He shook spumes of snow from its dead flowers.

He waded a mile towards the oak wood.

His first snare was untouched – rope taut and sapling flexed as he had left them. The same sight awaited him at the next. A third had a squirrel snared about the midriff. Death and the cold had stiffened it. Pink haws of blood lay in the snow where it had struggled.

Andagin untied the squirrel. Mere scraps, yet he gave it thanks for giving what it had. He inspected the russet fur to assess its condition. He took off his pack and extracted the cordage. He trimmed off a length with his knife and bound the squirrel by its neck to the strap of his pack. He swung the pack over his shoulder, feeling the sway of the corpse behind him.

He inspected his fourth snare at the woodland edge and found that one of the nooses had come undone. He set to replacing it and soon his eyes were so fused to the running knot, his mind so bound up with it, that it took a gasp to break his concentration and name that shape as it burst, in a spatter of snow, from cover.

A hare. Sprinting to close open ground. Passing so near he fancied he could see the ember of its soul rushing to catch up with it.

Andagin's heart pounced and his body followed. Already the bow was in his left hand, an arrow in the right, its flights crushed between his fingers and the haft.

The hare was quick – it leapt into a bank of heather. Andagin watched for tremors that might break the crust of snow. He began, with arrow poised, to close in on its hiding place. He let his feet do the thinking. Snow and brittle winter grass creaked beneath him. Closer each step, his eyes bridging the heather and the blunt tip of his arrow. It was like a raindrop on the edge of a leaf – at any instant the bond would break. Now. Or now. He trailed his foot in the snow. He stamped the ground.

The hare broke cover. It bolted and his arrow followed. He was in that flight. He felt it strike and the hare leapt as if the ground were a snake rearing up to bite.

The hare was not dead but knocked awry. Andagin gave chase, the animal in his chest hammering against its cage of bone. The hare stumbled, thwarted by a modest bank of earth. He saw, or thought he saw, the white blizzard of its terror as he fell upon it.

He was in the snow, his arms full of kicking muscle and tendons and fur. He managed to kneel and the snow was churned up and there was blood in it. He gripped the hare between his knees; more than its teeth, he feared those amber eyes. He hooded them with his hands and wrenched up and sideways. The hare shuddered. Andagin shut his eyes and swallowed his cry of triumph lest it spoil the gift.

He contemplated the hare in his lap. The light passed out of it. It was his duty to witness this, and not merely in beasts. He recalled the efforts of his aunt to be gone, the fever-light sharp in her eyes when he was brought to tell her goodbye. She had tried to touch his face and he remembered Judoc's grip on his nape preventing him from shying away.

Other deaths were not to be witnessed. His grandfather had walked one frozen night into the heath. Men found the corpse and took it to the hill fort for burning. Andagin had wept at the flames, though his mother told him that life had two gates and both led into the world.

Was this true? Had he walked the heath before as another? Would he again? He poked with his finger at the dead hare. If only he could see its spirit run on into the heather. Into the earth, like a seed in darkness to germinate there and rise again.

His father would cross that threshold soon. Andagin

would have to keep his face strong as they lit a pyre in the place of ancestors. The lintel of their house would fall and who but he remained to keep the other timbers from following?

His mind left the wood. It flew like a roosting crow to his father's sickbed. He saw the ribs stark in that ruined chest. Saw his father's roiling eyes as the coughing hacked him. And Judoc had turned against them all. Had they not been taught to walk their anger until it was spent: to shed a grievance on the heath and mark the spot of release with a stake plunged into the ground? Yet his brother disappeared for days without explanation. He seemed to crave his heart's burden. He let the rage walk him.

Andagin squirmed the pack off his shoulders. She beckoned to him. She promised him comfort.

His fingers fastened about Her stone. He brought it to the light and held it to his nose. There was lightning locked inside. He rolled the stone in his palm to give it the heat of his body. The likeness turned to flesh against his flesh. Opening his hand and lifting the stone to his face, he traced with his thumb the indentations, the beads about her breast and crown.

She had come to him, catching his eye where she lay among dull flints. She alone among the stones had spoken.

He raised the figure to his lips and breathed on her as if stone could thaw or kindle. He knew that the likeness was a prayer in stone. His friends collected flints and some of these were thunderstones which had cooled and kept their shape. The arrows of heaven. Yet his talisman fitted his palm and was more precious, for no thundercloud had forged it. Another than him had sensed the presence within and released it from bondage. Those hands had failed or forgotten: she had been lost, or escaped, to lie in wait for another. For him. For Andagin.

The chatter of fieldfare returned him to the day. Last snowflakes drifted like white bees above the heather. He stowed the stone in the pack, slung the hare over his shoulder and followed his bow into the wood.

———————

Alone for a spell – a breath of respite – Marcus Severus stood on the battlements and contemplated the day. Snow still fell in gusts, yet the bronze disc of the sun was attempting a breakthrough and where, to the south, it had burned a breach in the cloud, the stubble-pricked snowfields and frozen dykes gleamed.

It was a relief, after weeks of leaden skies, to see light again. Saturnalia was past, the worst of the darkness with it, yet this supposedly temperate island creaked in winter's vice. Marcus felt the cold in every inch of his being. Stamping his boots and slapping his biceps, he turned to survey the orderly grid of leather ridge tents and, beyond these, the bedraggled huts, the random smoke and disorder of the natives. A useless tribe, his superiors said: obstinate, dull-witted and indolent. Yet they had built long ago the earthworks above which he stood and the foundations of a city to come. Signs of progress were everywhere. Already, beyond the young orchards and cleared scrub, the circle of an amphitheatre had been scored into the earth. Posted as he was above the east gate, the decurion could send his eye along the straight flight of the new road.

'You'll get the measure of the place,' his commanding officer had said as they dressed in the unfinished bathhouse. 'It's all rain and thistles. They boil mutton till it tastes like old boot. And don't look for action in these parts. They've been tame for a hundred years.'

Aulus Pomponius Capito had been with the Legion when the rebel queen was vanquished. Four months into his posting, Marcus could not counter with similar experience. Aquitaine had been a soft province, yet he knew that country folk altered little with the climate. He was familiar with gossip and low cunning, the superstition that knitted fertility dolls from wheat stalks and hung the corpses of crows from the branches of wayside trees. He was a countryman himself, as the centurion never tired of reminding him:

'To a wheat weevil like you, this heath must look blasted. Its dismal hills. Its useless soil. A wet desert.'

'In winter, perhaps –'

'You've not lived through summer here. It so pelts with rain your feet start to rot. I've never waded through mud like I did last year.'

Marcus had learned all he cared to about the suppression of the revolt, yet he listened with every semblance of interest to his superior's account of the horrors that met the Legion: the noblewomen with their severed breasts sewn into their mouths, the veterans skewered in their fields as offerings to a savage god. Aulus Pomponius described, with relish, how the insurgents used barbed arrows to increase the difficulty of extraction, how they daubed the points with grease and animal blood and wrapped the shafts with fibres to contaminate a wound.

'Savage bastards. Wiping them out was a joy for us, like killing horseflies. I tell you, it's a good thing their cunt of a queen did herself in. There wasn't a soldier in Britain who wouldn't have taken his turn with her till her guts ruptured …'

Alone on the rampart, Marcus shook the centurion from his thoughts. He noticed that he had failed to scrape a smear of mud from his ankle and was bending to rub it off when he saw, through a lattice of stairs and crossing points, his servant in the forecourt.

Condatis climbed the steps, watching that he spilled nothing from his bowls and flagon.

Marcus took his breakfast and Condatis began to prise open oyster shells with his knife.

'I have been admiring our road.' His servant looked up, attempting to gauge what was required of him. 'It is not like your sandy paths. Your wayfarer routes that twist and turn.'

'My people,' said Condatis, 'do not see as yours do. We are not so here to there. We turn,' he said and, defeated by language, traced a snail's shell in the air.

The veins showed blue beneath the man's pale skin. He was lean and wiry; the grey hairs on his scalp were too sparse to be limewashed into a warrior's mane. He handed over the shucked oysters.

'My nurse used to warn me about your people. She liked to frighten me with tales of the dreaded Keltoi who once sacked Rome.'

'Long ago,' said the Briton in his own tongue. The decurion had learned enough of it to understand. It was hard to square the horrors of the uprising with this mild man. Marcus regarded that bowed head. The dwelling-place of the soul. To take a head in battle was to possess the soul of one's enemy – did they not believe that?

'Rome's past is your past,' Marcus said in the language of Rome. 'Do you not think it a glorious heritage to have come so close to the seat of your enemy?'

'My people are herders. We know nothing of old wars.'

'That is deftly spoken. Rome's peace will absorb your people. Our gods were the vanguard. Is not your Taranis our Jupiter in a local guise? And your Camulos is, I think, no match for our Mars.'

Marcus contemplated his manservant. There was strength in that leanness. Would he be of use as a guide in the hunt? Aulus Pomponius had plans to stir the blood by spilling some.

'Do you hunt, Condatis?'

'Hunt?'

Marcus spoke the local word – or what he took it to be. The tribesman blanched. 'The killing days are over.'

'You misunderstand. I mean for meat. Hunting beasts.'

Marcus hesitated. A local's sense of the land might help but not, perhaps, the local reverence for brute nature. It was good to set one's wits against a quarry – to boast over its flesh as if in victory. Why speak softly to a carcass, why thank its spirit that had none?

'What sort of man was your father?'

'A good man, sir. He died when I was young.'

'Was he a religious man?' Again, that muted bewilderment. 'Did he fear the gods?'

'Who does not fear the gods?'

'And the wild places, did he revere them? I have heard of a British man who ran mad when the Legion felled a grove of oaks.'

'I know nothing of this.'

'No, you are very tactful.'

Condatis had put on a cape of evasion. Marcus regretted his interrogation and wanted to share something of himself, to make a peace offering. 'My father is still alive. As far as I know. His trade is tableware. He sells to ambitious men who want their wealth to speak for itself.' The Briton nodded, secure in his deferential burrow. 'My brother stands to inherit the foundry and the business. I have soldiering. Perhaps it will keep me here, in your country.'

'It is your country now.'

Ah, thought Marcus, I have lured you out. 'Well, I will be pensioned off to fatter pastures. In the midlands, no doubt, where I shall dig turnips until another uprising finishes me off.' He sensed his servant weighing these words, sifting them for a nugget of intention.

'When that time comes,' the Briton said, 'perhaps you will consider my services.'

Marcus felt his lips open and close. 'Perhaps,' he managed to reply.

Condatis bowed and took back the breakfast vessels. Marcus watched him withdraw, negotiating with hands full the narrow wooden steps to the camp.

A raven cronked from one of the granary towers. Marcus looked for it through the smoke and growing clamour of the settlement. He noticed that the snow had stopped falling. It would be a bright day for once; all the better because unlooked for. A blessing.

2

No Man's Land

She realises only after she has woken that she did so braced for the smell of smoke on her pillow. The bedroom is hot and whiffy like a sickroom in summer, and the heavy curtains admit a sliver of breeze in which she expects, almost avidly, the scent of wildfire.

She lies on her back, looking at the spines of Polish thrillers on the bookshelves. Shutting her eyes, she wills sleep to reclaim her, but she is cut adrift and washed ashore on another day.

She gets up from the hardness of the bed and pulls back the curtains. A bright morning, another one, the sky pale blue and slashed with contrails. She fights with the stiff latch and lurches out –

– blossom and earth and cut grass. The neighbour leaning on the frame of his lawnmower. No smoke, at least not yet. She pads to the bathroom, pees, then goes downstairs. In the kitchen she finds a note folded and propped up against one of her grandfather's ashtrays.

Gone out on fire watch! Dad xx

She stares at the words as if she expects them to rearrange themselves on the paper. He has left her again to her home-work and the heavy tutting of the kitchen clock.

Bobbie slouches, slack-bellied, at the sink and looks out at the garden. The oaks are naked but elsewhere it's leaf-burst, the beech and chestnuts incandescent with spring. What her father calls the green mist. He wrote about it for the book he was working on before Mum left, before they came to Bagshot these Easter holidays to sort through fifty years of stuff – files, folders, clothes, books, pictures, furni-ture, garden tools, dusty junk in the garage. She wanders into the sitting room, barefoot on the worn carpet, and contemplates the cardboard boxes left open and gaping. When her father isn't filling these with his inheritance – though some are marked 'Mum', 'Roberta', 'Dump' – he is out on the heath. Why should she wait for him if he cannot be bothered to greet her when she rises? It's not as if there are DVDs to watch, or music worth listening to in her grandfather's record collection.

Bobbie returns to the kitchen. She pulls the dry loaf from the bread bin, hacks at it with the breadknife and fills the ticking toaster. Her friends will be playing in their North Oxford gardens. They will be cycling in University Park or going shopping with their mums. She has no one to hang out with. Only the Lost Boys. She imagines the heat coming off the sand on the Poors Allotment. Waiting for her toast, she pictures the journey – imagines setting herself against the hill, the soil clenching beneath her boots.

───────

A sunburst – a flashbulb going off in his face – and the air pulses. The noise is a giant punching him in both ears. Then (but there is no sequence, it's all now) the hot splash of shrapnel. He lies on the ground with the high, shocked whine in his ears. He feels but cannot hear the patter of dust falling. Someone is screaming.

He is on his back, waving his legs in the air to restrict blood flow. His heart isn't so much pounding as taking one. Air escapes his lungs –

– ah!

He's in bed.

He's in bed. He eases himself down and the sheets are damp with sweat. He focuses on his breathing – in through the nostrils, out through the mouth. Something catches in his throat and he hacks it loose, trying to do so quietly.

He reaches for his watch on the bedside table. 7:39. The Rev will be up, all cheery and wholesome and unfuckable in her kitchen.

He swings his legs over the side of the bed and the floor is cold and that feels good. He's in England. He's almost home. Almost back.

Ten minutes and a crafty fag later, he is dressed and kitted out at the breakfast table. Rachel is sitting behind her second or third cup of coffee. He can see on her face how he must look – wired and worn out at the same time.

'What's it today?' he asks.

'Wednesday. Holy Communion. You're most welcome.'

'Na, it's all right.'

She has left out the Rice Krispies and a sweating bottle of milk. The Rev sees but never mentions his shaking hands. She's careful not to slam doors and to set the volume low on the radio and the television so they don't come on with a blast. Even so, she makes mistakes. Like that time she invited him into the kitchen when there was raw lamb mince on the chopping board.

'You wouldn't care,' she says, 'for a grapefruit?'

'Uh …'

'This has been languishing in the fruit bowl. It's on my conscience.' She holds the grapefruit as he would hold her breast. 'I bought it in a fit of healthy-mindedness. Can't face it now.'

'Bitter.'

'I could manage it with a liberal sprinkling of sugar but I fear that would be missing the point.'

The Rev gets this way with food. Some people need things to feel guilty about. 'I don't fancy it,' he says. He sloshes milk into his breakfast cereal, hears it pucker and snap. He doesn't fancy this, either, but he needs to get something inside him.

'Rough night?'

'Why, d'I wake you?'

Rachel shakes her head. Sneaking a peek in her room that time, he saw the earplugs lying bent and mottled on her bedside table. 'Have you given any thought,' she asks, 'to my suggestion? I have that number at Veterans Aid.'

'I'm not a charity case.'

'Aitch, you literally are right now, and you're welcome, but staying here is no life, is it?'

'You want me to leave.'

'That's not what I'm saying.'

'Sounds like it.'

'You can stay as long as you've nowhere else, but we need to come up with a long-term plan. Where do you see yourself, three-four years from now?'

'Dunno, dead?'

'You don't mean that.'

'All right, stacking shelves, driving a forklift truck, working in a call centre selling shit to people who don't need it.'

'In a home of your own. Maybe with a partner, a kid.'

'I don't want kids.'

'Fine.'

'I'm not having kids.'

'Aitch, I'm being hypothetical. My point is, organisations exist to help people like you.'

'I'm dealing with it.'

'You scream in your sleep. You get up looking like you've been on a three-day bender and I know you haven't, it's just what sleep has done to you, it's what your dreams have done to you. There's nothing wrong with accepting help.' Her plump hands cup her mug of coffee that has COFFEE written on it. He stares at them because he feels the pressure of her watching and there's no way in the world he can push his eyes up to meet hers. 'Tell me you'll think about it.'

'Right.'

'Is that a yes?'

'Yeah.'

'I can do all the preliminary work – the talking, the forms ...'

Christ. She lifts her mug to drink and he feels the weight of her attention lift, so he looks up and sees red hair and the pink of her face, and in the garden the apple blossom is getting picked apart by the wind and he has to get out, into the woods. He looks directly at her, and if only he could pin her down on the table, his thighs slapping against her bare arse, pounding her till she shouts his name like it's not a sad puppy.

'Thank you,' she says.

'What for?'

'For being willing to listen.'

'It's your house.'

'Technically it's not.'

Aitch fiddles with his shemagh, drapes it across his shoulder. 'Reckon I'll go see Bekah,' he says.

'Is that wise?'

'Stu's at work. Then maybe I'll go for a run.'

'Okey-doke,' says Rachel. She drains her mug, gets up and puts it in the sink. Job done, parishioners to see. 'Will you be going through the heath?'

'Eh?'

'To your sister's?'

'Yeah.'

'It's just the ground's very dry. We're supposed to take care not to drop cigarettes.'

'"Don't burn everything, Aitch!"'

Rachel hiccups a laugh. 'I don't mean that.'

'Cross my heart, Rev, hope to die, I promise I will not burn down the heath.'

———

Locking the front door, she tastes the air. Nothing but the exhalation of flowers and, fainter, diesel fumes from a ride-on mower. She walks to the junction with College Ride. Putting Bagshot behind her, she follows the holly hedge as far as Pennyhill Park Hotel and its pungent hinterland of skips. At the crest of the hill she turns right, scaling a low bank of gravel shored up by oil drums. She pushes through holly and laurel, looking out for dog mess underfoot or bagged and hung from branches.

In the wood the footpath is obstructed with logging debris. Someone has been grubbing up rhododendron, leaving the wrack snagged in trees as if deposited by a great flood. She walks among roots and torn branches. Machines have carved deep ruts in the mud.

She drags a stick through the skeletons of last year's bracken, knocking tentacles of new growth. Everywhere the understorey is in leaf – rowans with their stems nibbled by deer, birches spangled with sunlight. A blackbird, threshing leaves in search of springtails, flies scolding at her approach. Birds seem to call from every corner – chaffinch, robin, wren – and she imagines their song as silver threads tying up the wood. Above the trees the sky is raw with the rasp of jet engines.

Bobbie enters the beech plantation. Her father has shown her the damage done to it by deer and squirrels. Inattentive, she treads in a rare puddle and tiny insects rise like vapour about her ankles.

Has she ever known the woods this dry this early? She thinks about the fire on the ranges. They were in the Vauxhall at the time, taking more of Grandpa's stuff to the dump. 'That's smoke,' her father said. The air flashed blue and they bumped onto the verge to let a fire engine pass.

'Could be a bonfire,' said Bobbie, seeing the expression on her father's face.

'It's not a bonfire.'

After that, he swerved as he drove because he was fiddling with the car radio to find a local news station. He swore at Dolly Parton, he swore at travel updates.

When they got back to Grandpa's house, he left Bobbie in the hallway and ran to fetch his iPad. The heath in Pirbright was in flames. Sparks, they reckoned, from ordnance or a soldier's cooking fire. Her father was scrolling in a sweat. 'Says here a thousand acres.'

'Is that a lot?'

'That's *the* lot. Jesus.'

It was because of drought, he said, and the winter dieback. Spring is the worst time of year for it – nestlings in the heather eaten by flames, lizards cooked on the blackened soil. Bobbie listened but she failed to make the necessary noises. It made her father sullen all evening.

She picks at shreds of bark torn from a beech by a gnawing squirrel. He reckons she doesn't care about the land, but that's not true. Didn't they come here every summer, and every autumn half-term, to endure Grannie's cooking and Grandpa's lectures? And weren't things easiest on those visits when all together they took off on long hikes, picking blackberries in August and mushrooms in October? Sometimes they found *Sparassis*, or brains as Bobbie calls it, spongy growths from pine stumps that you bake in casseroles or use to flavour omelettes. Deep amid the trees, they found boletus mushrooms with slimy caps. Best of all were the cep, so mild and nutty, filling her grandparents' house with the smell of autumn woods.

Those were among the few occasions when her grandfather, who considered the kitchen to be his wife's domain, commandeered the means of production and banished the family to the sitting room, summoning them with a crier's voice to *grzybowa* or mushroom soup, with poppy seedcake that he'd ordered from a Polish shop in Hounslow. That soup, Bobbie thinks, is lost to them now. Her father never learned how to make it – he's tetchy about picking mushrooms for ecological reasons – and Grandpa was not one to write his recipes down.

She sits on a stump among sweet chestnuts. The chestnuts are warped and dying, their flanks blackened by fire. Bobbie drinks from her water bottle and the cold makes her teeth ache. She lowers herself into stillness as her father taught her, trying to expand her peripheral vision – casting a web of attention to see what lands in it. She hears aircraft noise, traffic on Nine Mile Ride and the A30. Nearer, fainter, there is the shaken bell of a robin, the breeze in the pines. She tries to give herself to this moment, to stake a claim in it, but there are human voices at the edge of hearing and her wide-eyed stare contracts. She perceives, so dimly it might be a twinge of gristle in her jaw, the squeak of bicycle brakes. She stows the water in her rucksack and

touches as she does so the patterned stone in its inner
pocket.

She retrieves the stone. It soothes her to roll the familiar
shape in her palm.

Her father found it twenty years ago – long before she
existed – on a dig at Silchester. She imagines him with a
full head of hair, on padded knees in a trench, scraping off
the dirt with his thumbnail. The stone is shaped like a
withered pear and carved with ribs and pockmarks. It was
never knapped to kill or cut – its markings are odd, with
hatchings like decoration about what Bobbie thinks of as
its waist and neck. It's impossible to guess its age – it might
have been carved by a schoolboy on a field trip, or a soldier
resting on manoeuvres. Bobbie likes to claim it's prehis-
toric. No roads back then. No England. Only foraging and
hunting, small groups of people your only shelter and
hope of survival. When he presented her with the stone,
her father had been circumspect. 'I can't guarantee that it's
of archaeological interest.' Even so, it matters that the
stone is hers, that it came into her keeping. In the first
hand that held it, it would have felt the same as it does in
hers.

She puts the stone in her left trouser pocket and picks
up the footpath towards Surrey Hill.

Here he is, slouching behind the sports hall of the country
park hotel. There's gash everywhere: smashed beer bottles,
cans of Red Bull, plastic bags with dogshit inside. It's a
relief to get under the trees. In the beech wood there's a
girl, or maybe a boy, of ten or so, thrashing old bracken
with a stick. He doesn't often see kids here, mostly dog
walkers and lads from the estate on their way to the pub.

This path was one of his favourites on the Yamaha, taking turns with Donnie to punish their guts on its roots and stones. On foot, the gradient is starting to cost him. How can he be short of breath already? He's seriously out of shape. Not that the weather helps. Never known an April like it. Still, chilly after Helmand.

Ten litres a day he got through at first, the water warm and tasting of bottle plastic. Sweating like a pig out in the ulu. His arse-crack like a river. Mid-summer it got so hot his brain went numb. He only wanted to sit and breathe, and even that was like sucking the air inside an oven. But there were duties to perform, orders to keep them knocking about while the heat squeezed the sweat out of him and even the flipflops were sitting it out in their hovels, waiting for nightfall.

He makes it to the top of the hill. Twenty-three and he can still hack a bit of exercise. A few more paces and the trees give way to patchy scrub. He trained on land like this in Germany, but the sand and soil were no preparation for Afghanistan, its thin dust a powder over everything – in his skin, his hair, the parts of his rifle. Some days the dust was a beast, surging up in the downdraught from a chopper as if it wanted to smother it. Like the brownout when the Slick came for Chris and Gobby.

Who washed the dust out of their wounds? Did some of it travel home in their plywood coffins?

Fuck it – he lights a bine.

What is he going to say to Bekah? What arrangement of words can he come up with that would change anything with his sister?

He walks across the Poors Allotment, treading down the heather, dropping ash into it. He sees the burnt-out car, its rusted hull pierced by birch saplings. Strangely comforting that, knowing even the ugliest things will disappear. Or maybe that's wishful thinking. What could grow out of him to obscure the sights in his head? They come at him in the day but worse at night. Sometimes, too anxious to sleep, he walks up and down Church Road or into the dark of the forest. Last Saturday, after pub closing, he kept going along the A30 as far as the golf shop on Jenkin's Hill. Stood in its empty car park thinking: top spot for a sniper, you can see a mile down the road.

He is level now with the telecoms tower. It stands behind gates and razor wire, though it wouldn't be hard to get in if the fancy took him. He drops his fagbutt on the gravel and crushes it under his boot-heel. Has a quick sniff of his armpits. Tests his breath. She won't chuck him out if he pongs, not without a second reason. Still, a man has his pride.

In the Old Dean estate, people are either at work, asleep, or plonked in front of breakfast TV. Plenty of curtains are drawn and there's nobody about on the pale grass between houses. Outside Bekah's block he looks for Stu's van, but it's not there.

He rings the buzzer and waits a long time. Probably she's trying to pick Annie up, or yelling at Barry to turn his music down.

'Hello?'

'Bekah, it's me.' The intercom breathes static. 'Can I come up?'

She lets him in and he goes slowly up the stairs. The echoey landing, the dead tomato plants outside 2C, then ARCHER, Stu's surname where theirs used to be.

Bekah has put the latch on. He steps into the hallway that smells of last night's supper and the nappy bin. There are noises from the utility space, where he finds Bekah putting a load on while Annie sits playing with an empty bottle of Fairy Liquid. His sister presents him with a hard, perfumed jaw to kiss. His niece pays him no attention – she knows Aitch has nothing for her.

'You didn't tell me you were coming over.'

'It's not exactly far. Where's Barry?'

'How should I know?'

'Stu's at work, is he?'

'Where else would he be?' Bekah closes the drum of the washing machine and selects the economy cycle. Annie has shaken a drop of soap from the bottle and is spreading it with her foot on the lino.

'I'm parched – can I get a glass of something?'

'We're out of squash.'

'Tap's fine.'

Aitch escapes to the kitchen and pours himself a glass. He does a quick recce in the drawers and finds a pack of fags under some fliers. He shakes it at her when she comes in. 'Silk Cut? That's like inhaling air.'

'Oi, thief.'

'When d'you start on these?'

'I haven't,' says Bekah, 'they're just in case.'

'In case you give up?'

'Go on, you can have one.'

'Hardly worth it.' Yet he scrabbles for a cigarette and steps out on the balcony to smoke it. A hand appears behind him and shuts the French window.

When he's down to the filter, he flicks the butt to the pavement and knocks for readmission. Bekah has made a brew and he sits beside her in the living room, Annie squatting on her heels making marks on the Etch A Sketch.

'You just come to say hello?' asks Bekah.

'As opposed to?'

'As opposed to having news. Job interviews, getting on benefits.'

'I'm not a scrounger.'

'Neither am I, but I take what's owed to me and the kids.' Bekah pushes a plate of chocolate Hobnobs his way. 'So there's nothing?'

'Can't I just come for company?'

'Course you can.'

'When Stu's at work.'

'He's not gonna stop you calling.'

'He stopped me living here.'

'Don't start.'

'I wasn't taking up much space, was I?'

'Harry, it was like having a fucking black hole in the living room. You sat around all day looking depressed.'

'I needed something to do.'

'Yeah and you got it.'

The stacking job at the Co-op. Long days under neon. Christ, it was bone. But it got him out of the flat, out of Bekah's hair. Till he decked a punter who startled him with a question about broccoli.

'I'll get myself sorted.'

'How?' Bekah stares at him. 'What's different, what's changed since you were stoned on that sofa playing Xbox and watching …?'

She can't say it: filth. 'You don't think I can hack it.'

'Course I do.'

'No you don't. You think I'm fucked for life, some wreck with a Rupert in his head telling him he's shit.'

'What are you talking about?' His little niece begins to whine. Bekah picks her up and Annie pats her mother's face, almost slapping it. Bekah carries her into the bedroom and he can hear the quack and jingle of some kids' cartoon. She comes back at him. 'What are you talking about, a voice in your head?'

'Forget it.'

'That's not good, Harry.'

'Don't call me Harry.'

'Why not?'

'I don't like it.'

She stares at him. He looks for somewhere safe to bury his eyes. 'Don't you think you should see someone?'

'Christ, if I'd known it was gonna be like this I'd have stayed in bed.'

'Why'd you come and see me then?'

He looks at her feet that are swelling over the edge of her grey pumps. Her ankles look grey, elderly. 'I thought I could stay for lunch. Take Annie to the playpark. I don't mean on my own – obviously you'd be there.'

In the bedroom his niece laughs and shouts 'dog, dog'.

'I'm only doing spaghetti hoops,' says Bekah.

'That's OK.'

'Then I have to put her down for her nap.'

'I won't stop you.'

'I'll just go and check on her.'

Even now he can't talk to his sister. Like on tour, when he got his twenty-minute phone call. Standing there hearing the kids in the background and Bekah asking how he was, what it was like, and him thinking, I saw three men get vaporised in a drone strike, we held a memorial service in the cookhouse for a teenager from Crawley, I'm scared I'll bottle it next time there's a contact. None of this would have made sense back home, so he told her it was hot and Gobby sent his love and how were the kiddies, how was work?

The front door opens and he's off the sofa before Stu has put his toolkit down. It's as if he can smell Aitch, coming straight into the living room with his long snarky face. 'Wasn't expecting to find you here,' Stu says.

'All right, mate.'

'Where's Bekah?'

'With Annie.'

Stu is lean, a greyhound of a man, but he fills the room. 'How's things with the trendy vicar?'

'All right.'

He looks at Aitch down his long nose. 'She's relaxed with your mess, is she?'

'She's not up my arse like some RSM, if that's what you mean.'

'She let you up her arse yet?'

'Fuck off, Stu.'

'Single woman, strapping young bloke under her roof. Sounds like something you'd watch on telly. Mind you, a lady vicar – she's probably a lezzer.'

'If all blokes were like you, who could blame her?'

Stu wets his lips, grins. 'Good to see you, mate. Staying long?'

'Just came to see Bekah.'

'Yeah, well you seen her now, ain't ya.'

His sister returns with Annie on her hip. 'Dada,' Annie cries and casts off from her mother into Stu's arms. He makes a big show of kissing her cheeks and the tip of her nose.

'I wasn't expecting you back,' Bekah tells Stu, and the lack of warmth in her voice cheers Aitch up.

'You know me, efficient worker. I see we got the pleasure of a guest for lunch.'

'Na,' Aitch says, 'it's fine.'

'You're welcome, mate.'

'I got things to do.'

Bekah protests, or feels the need to pretend to. Even so he can tell she wants him gone.

'You give my best to Barry, yeah? See you, Annie. Stu. Bex …'

3

The Heave

First come our boy Malk.

He hold the guidin stick, it bein his turn.

He hold Abans knife. The knife they take off Feo in the bad time.

Feo they slaver beat Malk so black Aban so blue one night they bled him like a porker.

Runnin ever since with the blade that done it.

Malk reckon a knife done red work cut a way for us. Stedders smell blood keep out its way an the way its people. Cant say for hoofers but they go sly an void the roads cos they gods say so.

Aban talk bout the roads. The Thirsty with its robbers. The Empty where stedders have they tolls. So many dangers on our way to West Cunny. West Cunny where the rains still fall. Where Malk Aban Efia Nathin Becca Rona Lan headin. The pastures there. Tight bellies plus an end to roamin.

Fastest ways the road, say Malk.

Walk on till wind spew up sand an grit. Becca Lan pull they hoods tight. Nathin spit. Efia look at the spit, how Momma swallow it like she swallow everythin.

On the road, say Aban, trollers see for miles.

Yeah an we see em too.

Trumpet finches bust up from the dunes. Aban put a hand on Malks arm, feel the muscles there. His bro, his mate from wayback.

Safer ways off road.

Aint nuthin but scrub an sand. What if we lose us?

Follow the sun. Least we stay hid.

I got the guidin stick.

Whats it tellin?

Malk look like he dont know.

Efia touch Malks neck. Trollers mean slavers, she say. You got pricey heads.

Malk feel Aban Efia Nathin Becca Rona Lan press eyes on him. He turn the guidin stick in his hand, feel the right grain of it, true grain that know the way an give rightness to its holder. Off roads slow, he say.

Nuthin slow like never arrivin.

The group all gree when Malk lift the guidin stick. Then Becca say she thirsty. Whole groups thirsty, say Rona, an suns gearin up for a hotten. One hour since dayup an the sands bakin, the airs meltin an carders workin up they *skikishik*. Lan give Becca the dregs from her jercan.

In a kayshas shade we share beetle grubs cook in last nights ashes. Nathin give up three strips of jerk he bin keepin in his belt. The stink of jerk bring flies. We sit flappin our swats. Long wait fall on us then. No thinks, just breathin. Rest our eyes on the plain, all swimmy like water tho there aint none. Watch birds hangin up high, specks turnin to wild dog, camel, blackbuck.

We cant stay here, say Malk. Grubs low an water too. How fars the nearest well?

The Winnel, say Nathin. Bout an hour. Half at night.

Stedder place, say Becca. Why risk it?

Cos we jercans empty, say Rona.

Winshams close, say Nathin. Shop there after.

Can do, say Aban. Need fresh legs if stedders catch us.

Well it is, say Malk liftin the guidin stick. Hole up an wet throats till nightfall. Then we shop at Winsham.

In parch time a waterin place show from its palms an willows. We creep in slow, lookin out for stedders. Fresh earth smells. Hoopoes in the branches. Soil between our toes cool an sucky after sand an dust. Only mud tho so long the dry an stream gone underground. In wintertime a waterin place flood again or should do. Old wintertimes leastways before the rains fail.

The Winnel have three wells. Two in use by stedders but one near us just gapin sayin, Coo-yoo, wet yer beaks here.

We run to the well our jercans ready. Nathin Aban bend they backs to lift the bucket. Soon as done the group fan out lookin for things to eat. Lan find a ditch of slime boilin with frogs. We catch the frogs, stuff em in our packs, skewer em on sharpsticks. Good eatin if we risk a fire. Not tonight tho. Best eat raw. Keep out of stedders sight. Fat up our nerves for shoppin.

Lan put a snail on her tongue an all the group laugh. Malk take out the knife an start to skin frogs. Efia watch the bodies fall at his feet like squirmy little blokes.

Our jercans full, we hole up the day in a cork grove. Far enuf from hearin but close enuf to watch. Sussin out the doins on the Winsham palisades.

When shadows spread, Aban crawl out thru scrub an grass to the gate of the sted. He look round, see women poundin grain, carryin water on they heads. Sentries dozin in a cedars shade. Others nabberin by the meetin tree.

Creepin closer Aban find gaps in the fence, look at the market stalls. Suss out the grain store. Then snake an scrabble back to us.

Wassup, say Malk.

Hungers comin.

How so?

Winsham folk sellin goods an stocks. Fuelwood. Dung cakes. Nuthin blokes can sink they teef in.

Less blokes eat shit, say Lan.

What grains?

Sorghum. Maize. Meat too an cows blood.

Killin what they cant keep, say Rona.

The group turn quiet. Look into the trees so pictures in our heads stay hid. None of us as dont know the pain of hunger.

Abans first to bright up. Makes sense shop now then dunnit? Go in fast an quick.

Take what? You say theres nuthin sellin.

We aint buyin. Look they got grain stores on stilts. Keep rats an coons out give us nifty cover. Drill our way in.

Like in Whey Bitch, say Becca.

No, say Malk. This shop we get back. All on us.

What if some don't, say Becca.

We go nifty. Not like last once.

Sez you, say Becca an Rona hug her for quiet. Malk take his eyes off Becca slow an warnin.

Boys go, say Nathin.

Balls, say Rona. You shop grain stores we scout the sted. See whats goin.

An the sentries?

Run if we can fight if we cant. Malk take up his sharp-stick. On my signal, he say. Click an slick.

Slicks our movin. Clicks our speakin without words. All on us kneel in mud an black our faces.

When the sun cook like an egg on the ground, its time.
Hoods down. Turbs in place. Pray patches on our clothin.
Sit in our heads readyin for danger.

The sky hatch a fat moon. Nightspit on the grass an
spidie threads like smoke on the ground. Cool breeze good
as sleep after the blazin day.

Fires in the sted die out. Stedders go sleep in they huts.
Only sentries pacin over the gate.

Now, say Malk an we move. Like Aban before we shift
cross the plain to our bizness.

Malk bein strongest hoist us over. Lan Efia Rona Becca
hide next a pigsty but Aban almost land on a billy, it run
bleatin, bell janglin an Nathin go to split its throat but
Malk stop him. Goats get spook for nuthin, he say, leave
it be. Nathin nod tho his eyeballs dancin. Grains this way,
say Aban an he click, Upyer.

Aban wriggle under the grain store. Down in the dark
best not think on rats or spidies. Lan Efia Nathin follow
with packs open an Aban use the drill. Happen the floors
made of wood so he blow dust from his hands an spin till a
breakthru. Nuthin here so start again. An again. Fourth time
some grain come tricklin so he gouge hard with his sharpstick an out it come like steam. Aban shove fast now makin
holes an everyones sweatin, the sand an sawdust in our eyes,
our packs gapin *yorr* an gobbin up the spillin grain.

Outsight samewhile, Malk Rona Becca creepin bout the
sted seein what they find tho nuthin much, all lock up for
the night. Clothes dryin worth a trade. Some blokes hoe by
a wall, a pair of sandals, a clutch of piggly pears. Malk
Rona Becca drop when a watch pass nabberin too loud to
know shoppers near.

More clicks from Aban. Lan Efia Nathin scrape clear
of the grain store, packs bulgin. Malk Rona Becca scurry
to join us but Lans pointin, Look, an all look at lights
winkin an wavin in the huts. Lanterns movin in the
darkness.

Quick!

First Becca Rona jump over an fall *crump* on other side.
Aban next then Nathin but the crys up, the watch hollerin
an lantern lights nippin at our faces. Lan hop, she skip like
shes standin on hot sand an quick, shout Malk, *quick*, but
Lan run from the chasin lights. Malk reach out but grab
only the wind of her. Toss over his loot, his sharpstick, help
Efia an take a run after, splinterin his fingers, warpin his
nails to get over.

Other side of stockade its no use creepin. We run till our
hearts bash gainst our ribs. Back to the grove. Find others,
grab loot, get away from Lans cries.

Malk Efia tumble into the hidin place. Lost for thinks
we say nuthin, only Beccas sobbin.

Lets go, say Nathin.

No, say Becca.

Winshams got Lan now. They learn our hideyway then
come for us.

But Lan! You say we get back. All on us.

Malk say nuthin his head droppin but Aban see him
look his way. Too late, Aban say. They got her now but she
wont come to harm leastways not killin.

Forced hitchin, say Efia. Forced hitchin an sprogs till she
die of one in her upways.

Or grindin, say Becca, till some bloke pox her.

Shes *lost*, say Malk. Like us if we dont shift. You on yer
backs an Aban me kickin on a gibber.

Blokes voices on the plain. Lamps swingin, old church
bells dangin an all Winsham up searchin for us. No time

to say, Lan oh Lan, but uppin quick we check our packs an sharpsticks. Malk hand the guidin stick to Aban, nuthin sayin. Aban think before he take it but Malk push it an up it go in Abans fist.

We run cross scrub till dayup an stedders long gone back to bed.

———————

Scaldin light an sky like a furnace door left open. Hidin in a wood of yewkas after a fire, leaves still hangin like yellow petals. Becca Rona Nathin Efia. Nathin with the guidin stick case Aban Malk dont make it back. They gone to Bad Shot to shift goods. Hopin news of the raid on Winsham dont beat em to it. Becca Rona moanin, Lan oh Lan, till it get too hot for moans an they sleep. Nathin turnin over the guidin stick praise it, stroke its carvins. Efia search for grubs an locusts tho in her head too its, Lan oh Lan. The group grieve but Efia reckon she an the group not always the same an her pains sharper an deeper cos Lan was her best her closest since they kids together in Roil Wells. How they scape the same fate. Hitchin to old blokes. Old blokes with land an plenty of kids from the wives they bust up havin em. Tho they moms say thats just The Way they aint gonna walk it. Live free together. Live on the run. All lost now an broke.

Samewhile up north, Malk Aban take booty into Bad Shot. Aban tell all this later. Later when we share whats done. Bad Shot he says a richer sted than Winsham, its walls stronger an more stedders on count of Thirsty Roads traffic an trade. Richer the sted the more talismans outsight. Bad Shots got all see-see boxes with they bust up eyes an coily tails. Heads of crits on poles. Grass dolls hangin from rusty nails. Keep out if you mean bad. Malk

Aban mean good. Trade an scarper. No shoppin in Bad
Shot. No riskin any lives.

Wassup, bloke at the gate say. Malk Aban stand whiles
stedders frisk em an bung they snouts in our loot. Clothes,
a hoe, a pair of sandals, some grain. Aban note the stedders in cammo like juntamen. Two on the ramparts holdin
akays.

Hotten innit, say Malk but the stedders ignore him.
One, a heavy bloke with a bust nose an face tattoos, point
his cosh at him. Do you follow the Law, he say.

How so bro, say Malk.

How so you worship the Law yer maker an fear the
Law yer breaker.

Oh for show, say Aban, for show.

Bad Shots a loyal sted an a christun.

We trade, say Aban, only with christun folk.

The big bloke suck his teeth lookin at em. Dont sound
like hoofers, he say an gob over his shoulder. Biddy
welcome.

Cheers, say Malk but he walk into the blokes cosh. Hot
breath in his face an black eyes borin into him. Any grief,
say the bloke, an kites ul peck out yer eyes.

Makes sense dunnit, say Aban.

The Law have eyes an see you. Send fleshflies to blow
yer corse if you cross him. Malk Aban watch the cosh fall
an draggin the loot they enter Bad Shot under the akays
waitin muzzles.

Cheerful bloke, say Malk.

Cheerful sted, say Aban. Soon as done we best be off.

Rightyer, say Malk.

Bad Shot stink an swelt in the sun. Houses of tarp an
breezeblock from the Fast Time manshuns. Stedders in
white curters an jelabas. Women carryin water in bark
pots. Bowleg kids young as five heave they bros an sissies

on they backs. Smell of dead crits an donkey shit. Dogs skulkin for grub, cowerin gainst sticks or stones. More blokes in junta gear watchin from doorways. Aban whisper, Jorjes Army?

Malk shake his head. Long time since the junta send its army west. Boys find the market at a crossroads. Few stalls under canvas. Women pickin over dusty melons, piggly pears, roast locusts. Bunnies showin pink where they innards cut out, the bald flesh peppery with flies. Stedders eyes slide to the goods the boys carryin. Costin. Considerin. Aban find one stall got what they lookin for. What for a dewcloth, he ask the stall bloke.

What you got?

This hoe.

Bloke shake his head.

This hoe an these sandals.

Bloke or bitch?

Small bloke big bitch, say Malk an the stedder crack a smile. Got him now.

Bloke hand over a dewcloth. Know how to use it, he ask.

We know, say Malk. How bout plasters?

Some. You?

Malk Aban take out stole clothes but keep the grain hid in they packs. Stall bloke make a lemon suck face. For yer wife, say Aban. He tug out a yellow sari. Gotcha gain think Malk cos the blokes eyes bulge an, Maybe why not, he say, tryin too late to swallow his greedy look.

This for plasters an that bucket there.

Keep her smiling, say the stall bloke as he stow the sari out of sight. Where you boys from?

Whey Bitch, say Aban fast an easy. The Wen before that.

Wenners eh? Met a bloke once ran slave ships in Canny Wolf.

Dunno Canny Wolf, say Aban.

Tradin place innit. Where you headin?

Malk go shifty, look to move, but Aban play it fast. North, he say. Lookin for harvest work. No sooner the words loose than he want to catch em back cos the stall bloke frown an wall up gainst em. Best scapes forward, Aban think, an fearin a sweat on him he say, Wassup bro? North no good is it?

Dunno, say the stall bloke. Not up the Middens least-ways. Word is its steds vee hoofers like when you was lads. The bloke lean close, his fat arm in his wares. Hoofers like weeds, he say. Pluck em up an they grow back all over. Cos of the Dry see an folk what grow stuff claimin land off the lifestock.

So whats new, say Malk.

Its numbers innit. Breed like rats them hoofers. Loud enuf for half Bad Shot to hear the bloke add, Ousters most on em. Not christun folk thats for show. Lose animals in the Dry an they raid a sted. Stedders wont have it an why should they? Call on Jorjes Army. Back to axes an mashtis.

Nuthin stedders cant sort out, say Aban, wantin to go. Jorjes lot ul see it right.

Rightyer but they – The stall bloke lean in again an whisper. *They* bring trouble an all. Looters do. Rob good folk soon as bad.

Aban Malk give no thinks to this. Seein as we headin west, fightin in the Middens no fret of ours. Fact, worse things get the better, cos stedders watchin hoofers mean less eyes for us. Aban Malk go to leave but the blokes not done. Like he want to warn the boys.

Looters bad enuf, he say. But worse follow.

Like what?

Slavers. Blokes huntin fresh meat. Bounty men.

Aban burn on a sudden hotter than the day call it. He drop his grain pack.

If theres a price, say the stall bloke, after kids whats grown up runnin –

Not our prob, say Malk.

For show for show. Still an I mean watchyer. For bounty men a lookylikes good enuf. Theres prizes on all sorts of heads. Crims on the run. Scaped slaves. You name it they lookin. Not so many blocks on bizness when wars afoot.

The boys get away fast as clever. Did the stall bloke know em? Guess they story? Fast an nabber free they barter clothes for saltmeat, rope an bundles of tarp. Grain goes for bags of sorghum an maize. Supplies better than Aban see in Winsham but here too signs of hunger. One bloke in a side streets skinnin a dog strung up by its back legs.

What yer think, say Malk as they shoulder they packs. Bout slaver talk an bounty men?

Think nuthin, say Aban. Nor say nuthin till we far from this shithouse. Silent they walk under the gate where the sentries sit, scannin the Thirsty for signs of trouble.

———

Crawlin thru scrub longside the Thirsty Road. Keepin low case stedder patrols or juntamen see us. Packs on our backs. Sweat drippin from our chins an guts full but brains hungerin for shade. On, keep on. Till Rona Becca crump to they knees.

Upyer, say Malk.

Upyer own, say Becca.

Crits aint stirrin, say Rona. Birds shush. Even carders restin.

Aban offer his jercan but Rona shake her head an push it back.

So Nathin Aban scout off ahead whiles Rona Becca Malk Efia rest in sharp an furzy shade. Soon Nathin Aban come back.

Got a place, say Nathin. Up the hill an not far off. No blokes about.

One bloke, say Aban. But he wont say nuthin.

Up at the ruin off the Thirsty we all look up. The corse hang from the gibber in a halo of flies. Eyes et by crows, face black like a bad fruit. Efia look at the square of bark danglin from the dead foot. She can read tho no one else can.

They hang him, she say, for startin a bush fire.

Way to go, say Nathin.

Stinks an all, say Rona. Leave him to his thinks.

Becca take Efias hand. We cant stay here, she say. Not next to that.

Best place for us, say Malk. Smell ul drive blokes elseways. Bad luck an cross a workin gibber.

Its bad luck is bad on us too, say Becca. Cant sleep the night an him rottin just outsight.

Malk pull angry at the pray patch in his cloak. Look, he say. Alla Man give em to us. Magic powers in magic words from far off. Magic an the Laws word.

So, say Becca.

So we got cover. Words keep danger off.

An we think good on the corse, say Efia, puttin a hand on Beccas neck, corse think good on us. Right?

The group all gree till Becca stop her moanin.

Into the ruin we go. Nuthin but a dusty shell, tho cooler in than out. Some keep watch while others sleep. Efia sit with Aban. She look round the room wonderin if its a Fast Time manshun. Not built for now, thats for show. In Roil Wells back when she serve in a salt merchants house, it were tall an deep an dark, it were like a net to catch the breeze. Him an his wife baskin in it like fish in water. This ruin tho made for easy livin. No breeze holes nor ducts save whats done by time an weather.

Tell me, say Efia, what you see.

Aban shrug. He watch the road all slick like a river of heat. Sand each side like a cauldron simmerin. Land curvin off in a smudge of haze.

Efia drink from her jercan an Aban from his. Share some saltmeat an beetle grubs from the yewka grove.

Beccas fraid, say Efia.

Aint she always?

Rona keep her strong but she cant carry her all the way.

Dont worry bout Becca.

You reckon its true, say Efia. Bout the patch magic?

Dont you?

Dunno. Aint what I hold to.

Its what we got.

Efia Aban sit sweatin with no more thinks between em. So begin the Numb. Waitins not the word, for waitins a doin an the Numb dont act nor want neither. Its like gettin to be a stone. Or a lizard on a rock. Head empty an heart slow. No pictures, no sayin. All shut down till the heat drop. Wait without waitin for time to start again.

Aban stand when Malk Rona join us. Malk naked, his brown skin gleamin, scars like a map of rivers cross his torso. Efia see Malk hard. Rona fix him, Malk fix her back, her eyes black an sweat on her lip, her breasts bare, Lans necklace of shells tuck between em. No word sayin Efia stir beside him, she lift her shirt an Abans risin too. Efias breasts small, the nips dark an scars in rings bout her belly nub. Malk Rona curl like cats on the floor, Rona take Malk in her gob, Malk groan oh, an Efia bare now, her dress like a pool bout her feet, her feet specky with sand,

the slave brand like a half moon on her hip. Aban fix her
face, shes weepin Lan, an he lift his jelaba, smell of him
sheddin like a skin. Naked Aban go to Malk Rona trembl-
lin place his hands on Ronas head, Malk groanin. Efia
creep to bind Aban in her arms, her breasts gainst his back.
Some time after, the room blue with shadow, an Becca
come step over Rona Aban Malk Efia, step over us, see
into her, she squat an the stink of her, Efias black hair
tangle in Beccas red an Becca Efia Malk Rona Aban tangle
blue in moonlight an now Nathin come, Becca Rona part
to take him, he sink into the river of flesh, the one current
drag us all one, Rona Becca Aban Efia Malk Nathin, all
fuse writhin an bodies blue in moonlight an his on her an
my on his an Becca Rona Nathin Aban an Malk Aban an
Rona Aban oh Lan Aban Aban

Efia!

wake in belly of night, the moon set an the group flesh to
flesh. No sound but the trees only. Leaf whisper Efia take
at first for rain. Not rain tho. None for months now. She
lie with Rona pressin gainst her, the room smellin of sweat
an sleep an cum. The group smell. Becca lie curl up knees
gainst her elbows, gob open, corner of her thumb restin in
it. Cool at last. Cool that wont stay cos a new days heatin
up already out east where the days hatch, but for now a
breeze an hearin Efia shiver Aban grope for clothes, his or
hers or others, he crawl with the clothes an pull em gentle
cross her thigh an belly.

Aban feel to the window look out cross the black still
river of the road. See the lighter body of sand each side.
Star shadow of the gibber an its lonely corse. Feel the
breeze on his skin. More than the corse ul ever do. Live for
this. For the dark hours an the smell of night.

Light flickers in the web of trees. Like a star but not so high. Flicker again. Not one star but four or five. More than five. Like part of the nights come down to earth.

Malks beside him. Malks hand on his shoulder.

Bad Shot?

Aban shake his head. Closer, he say. Aban Malk lean half out like stoats sniffin the air, like crits peerin from a burrow. Fraid of the world an its hunger. Come, whisper Malk, an Aban follow cross sleepers into the house, up broke stairs all dusty an heaps of stuff too dark an smash to reckon. Into the room where Malk Rona Becca Nathin sleep out the hot time earlier. Aban grope in the dark but Malk know his way. To a window facin west. Still glass in this, leastways fangs of glass, the middle smash out long ago. Malk Aban look out cross the Thirsty Road, other side all the way to West Cunny. All our hopes there. An more lights strollin. Far off gainst trees a glow of flames. Mid the rain song of nearby trees they listen. Voices just. Grumblin of camels an horses cryin.

Stedders, say Aban.

Could be hoofers.

Middens too far off. More likely stedders. Or juntamen diggin in. Leastways Thirstys under watch.

Road go straight our way.

Till we get done. Load of trollers versus you me an Nathin? Walkin into bad lucks bedroom innit.

Sez you.

Full on campments Malk? Stedders in cammo an akays bout they necks? You see em in Bad Shot.

I see em.

Go low, say Aban. Cross country.

You fraid of slavers? Fraid we hang for Feo?

Fraid on lots of things Malk. Dayup soon. Best be off.

Cross scrub you reckon?

Elseways a dead way.

Livins a dead way. Only place we know we goin.

But not yet Malk.

No.

Not yet.

Malk nod. Thirsty Roads shut to us. Empty Road further souths a junta supply route.

Well before dayup the groups gone an melted into the heave.

4

Blueface

The canopy knitted above him, the bones of its oaks clattering and creaking in the wind. Andagin was not afraid. He knew how, after leaf-burst, the trees would transform into a green net to catch the sun. For now they slept, they whispered in their dreaming and he slowed his pace not to wake them.

In the midst of the wood there was a brook the colour of rust. He meant to try his luck there. He had a few hazelnuts in his pack but hoped it would be enough to break the ice and use the flowing water as bait.

He had not been long at setting new snares, the nettle string unspooled between his fingers, when he heard the snapping of branches. His first thought was to reach for his bow, but it took only a breath to gauge the size of what broke the quiet.

He strained to hear voices and knew from their cadence that these were his people. Footfalls cracked twigs, crunched in snow, and he watched through a veil of alders the familiar shapes of his brother and Barocunas and their cousin Lugh.

Barocunas was first, leaning his bulk into the undergrowth to fray a passage. Lugh, his ginger mane dusted with snow, appeared intent on explaining something which Judoc bent sideways to hear.

Andagin crossed the brook at a single bound. The noise startled the others, for as he skipped towards them, anticipating his cousin's wrestling embrace and a brotherly hand on his shoulder, he saw the young men stiffen.

'I am laying traps. I caught a hare.'

Lugh waved, not to greet him but to urge him back. Andagin faltered as Barocunas lumbered towards him.

'Are you spying on us?'

Andagin held out the cordage and knife. Barocunas inspected the objects as if unsure what to make of them.

'You must not follow us.'

'I was not.'

'We are just walking.' This did not account for the cold reception so Barocunas spoke again. Words seemed to cost him. 'We have things to do.'

'What things?'

'Our own.'

'Can I speak to Judoc?'

'No.'

'He is needed at home.'

Barocunas rested a heavy hand on the boy's skull. 'Go back to the heath. Lay your traps there. Stay away from the trees.'

Andagin watched his brother and the others walk away, into the fastness of the snowbound wood.

The cold was a mask on his face that made his tears sting. He hated himself for his weakness.

He waited until the trees and the hill had swallowed Judoc, Lugh and Barocunas.

Defiance and indecision churned within him. He felt them settle.

The hare would slow him down so he stowed it in the fork of a pollarded birch and covered it with dead bracken. The squirrel he broke and folded into his pack so that it would not snag.

The oak wood closed over his head like a wave.

It was easy to read the signs of their passage. One of the boys must have been swinging a stick, for the ruined lace of old bracken lay on either side of the milled snow. He listened out for voices, moving at a half run to make up lost ground. Then he faltered – for a line of unfamiliar prints joined those he was following.

He crouched to study these prints that came from the south, where the forest began. He discerned the feet of a man and the paws of a dog: a large one to judge from its pads. He spanned the place where the trajectories met, and wondered if this confluence of paths indicated a meeting or a pursuit.

He guessed the trail's endpoint. He saw the place in his mind: a grove older than memory, for yews outlive other trees and sprout anew from their rootboles. It was a place most people feared to visit. He told himself not to mind the stories Judoc used to frighten him with. These woods knew him: they would not let him come to harm.

No voice warned him of the boys' nearness. He had to drop like an acorn from its cup – for if he could see Barocunas and Judoc and Lugh, they could see him.

A man was with them. A man with a wolfhound at his side.

The man's clothes were the colour of earth. Their leather suggested tree bark, a forest hide. For a breathless instant Andagin saw a demon from the Otherworld come to claim its tribute of souls. Yet the stranger, when he turned to face those worshipful faces, looked human. The hair had

receded on his dirty skull and one leg was warped, as if it
had been broken and badly reset.

Andagin pressed into the leaf meal. He waited for the
waters of his courage to rise, then lifted his head.

The company stood outside the yew grove. The stranger
confronted its green ramparts with arms aloft, and even
with his back turned it was possible to discern the quaking
of that black beard. At his belt the man wore a sword,
although this was forbidden. A torc of tarnished bronze
hung about his neck.

Now, Andagin's heart told him. *Now*. He writhed and
scrabbled backwards until an oak shielded him. He forgot
his defiance. He wanted only to be back with Nyfain and
his mother and his dying da. The dread he felt – sharp,
rank, unfamiliar – frightened him in its intensity, and it
was only when his knees began to ache from the crouching
that he dared to look around the tree trunk at the entrance
to the grove.

They were in there. They had gone inside with that wild
being.

Andagin held the carved stone. He warmed it in his fist.
The stranger in the grove was frightening to think of.
Despite the cold, a sump of sweat welled in the small of his
back. If he were discovered, he might be sent home with a
buzzing skull.

He rolled the stone in his palm. He lifted it to his lips
and kissed it. He could not bring himself to leave the
wood, to obey the instruction of that bully Barocunas.

The grove beckoned.

His feet snagged on brambles. He crept closer and
sensed that something was in the trees behind him. Or did
he imagine it, for the rustling might be his own, a squirrel
perhaps, or a blackbird turning over frosted leaves. He
took another step, then a third.

The wolfhound was upon him. It pounced and the world tipped over. Andagin was on his back, his fingers full of fur. He felt the defencelessness of his eyes and nose and cheeks. He tried to scream but his lungs were robbed of air.

He heard the shouts of his kinsmen. The hound pinioned him with the great clubs of its forequarters. If he could fight it, but his knife was in the pack and the stone –

– the stone! He cried out, 'No, no!' and a second body was pressing against his. Andagin recognised the bronze torc, the black tangle of beard.

He shut his eyes as a callused hand covered his mouth.

He was back in his quarters when word came: tradesmen from the east leaning out of their carts, a dispatch rider from the broken city, hollering to the sentries about damage to the road.

Aulus Pomponius Capito intercepted the forecourt chatter and issued a plan of action.

Condatis brought Marcus his armour and sword and helmet. The decurion carried his own equipment to the stables. He kicked a stable lad in the straw and waited for his mount.

Soon, he was greaved and helmeted and patting his horse's cheek. He contemplated the inspection party under his command: the cavalrymen Lucius Agilis and Glyco, and Celer the engineer, who scowled at the cold and the temporary revocation of a civilian's autonomy.

'You look,' said Glyco to the engineer, 'like a mourner at your own funeral.' Glyco the Sicilian was, by reputation, a troublesome brute, much used by Aulus Pomponius to test the authority of his officers. 'We should be glad of the exercise. I for one am sick of living under hides. A brisk trot in the snow, a sniff round some broken pavings. Give me those over cracking fleas by lamplight.'

'Some of us,' said Celer, 'have works to oversee.' The engineer, a small man with large hands and skin the complexion of smoked fish, winked at the feeble light. 'We could do with more sun.'

'We could,' said Marcus. 'Here it comes, bottled.'

He had ordered Condatis to bring flagons of beer into the yard. The cavalryman Lucius Agilis made grateful noises, but Glyco, even as he drank, performed a mime of distaste.

Refreshment taken, the company prepared to depart.

'Here,' said Glyco. 'You ever seen a clerk ride a stallion?'

'No,' said Lucius Agilis.

'Here's your chance.'

The engineer's knuckles were white about the unfamiliar reins. 'Horseman,' he said, 'when you can keep twenty hundredweight of brick in the air, I'll await a demonstration.' He turned to Marcus. 'I had a dozen tasks today. Well, I know my place.'

'It's not on a horse,' said Glyco.

Marcus would have to watch that one. Lucius Agilis would give him less trouble. Twenty years under the Eagle had squeezed the juice out of the man. It was said that Lucius had served since the conquest and that a native woman was waiting for him to receive his pension. Marcus saw a man biding his time until freedom.

'Have your wits about you,' he said. 'We ride in tight formation. I anticipate no trouble but keep your eyes sharp. With a little luck, we should be home for dinner.'

How long had he been here – a captive – hearing whispers and footfalls? He thought it must be half a day, yet the light was young when the hood was pulled from his head.

He gulped cold air, half blind. Hands belonging to red hair and blue flesh brought water to his lips. It tasted of mud.

The hood was replaced. Darkness again and the itch of hemp. His hands were bound in his lap. He was tied by the bonds to a tree.

He dared not make a sound.

Voices were clearer now. He recognised that of his cousin Lugh. He did not think it possible to be more afraid than this. What he heard taught him otherwise.

'You speak tall,' said Barocunas. 'You speak like a warrior. But you have no parents living, only your fat aunt who used to beat you.'

'That sounds like fear.' This second voice belonged to Lugh. 'This is no deed for tender hearts. You can sit with your ma and your ugly sisters and let your spirits rot if you have no stomach for it.'

'Who can doubt that I have? Judoc? Have I no stomach?'

Andagin trembled to hear his brother speak.

'We are pledged,' Judoc said. 'Yet my heart fears for those I love.'

'Love makes us slaves. It is our duty to bring our hearts to heel.'

'Yet what will happen to them –?'

'The wolf does not pity the sheep. Our kin have no claim on us now.' Lugh spoke, his words hard as iron: 'Every day I see it. The fort is a shrine to our weakness, where the people meet to get drunk on foreign wine. You see noblemen clean-shaven, trying to look like their masters. Is this not so, Aesu?'

'Aye.' This was a new voice. Aesu, a friend of his brother's from the hill fort. A giant of a youth.

'And is it not true that your brother, who was prenticed to the blacksmith, is gone to the garrison town to ply his trade?'

'He has,' said Aesu.

'And your uncle, Judoc, has married his daughters to the enemy. Calleva brings the greedy and the scheming to it like flies to shit. No wonder the gods blast us. For want of a sacrifice I fear a bitter spring.'

'We are warriors,' Aesu said. 'The land is frozen but we shall thaw it.'

'Aye.'

'The gods look away but we shall turn their faces.'

'Aye!'

'We shall avenge the fall of Mona. We shall avenge the eastern queen.'

'Boys …' The voice was a wind that flattened all voices. 'My boys, the riders will be out. They are coming.'

Andagin strained to listen, as if by effort he might burn a hole in his hood.

'You are Taran's thunderbolts. Strike for me.'

There was a long silence before the sough of boots in snow. A body crouched beside Andagin and released him from darkness.

'Judoc!'

'Quiet.'

He saw a makeshift encampment, the ruins of a fire, a small tent made of hides strung among the yews. The bearded stranger watched him across the clearing.

'That man,' said Andagin.

'Drink some of this.' Judoc's face was painted and his hair limed into a horse's mane. He tipped a skin of bog water and Andagin drank, the wet slobbering into his lap.

'Untie me,' said Andagin.

'I cannot.'

Judoc took away the skin and produced a strip of salted meat. Andagin shook his head after two mouthfuls. 'It sickens me.'

'There is nothing else.' Judoc's chest moved as though he had paced over the brow of a hill. 'What were you *doing*? How could you be so *stupid*?'

'I am not the stupid one.'

'I can put this back on. Andagin, you are in terrible danger.'

'Whatever you are planning – whatever this is –' Andagin strained to look over his brother's shoulder at the black beard and the staring eyes. 'Oh, he is watching me.'

'No wonder. You have made him doubt us.'

'It hurts.'

'Why did you come then? Why did you follow us?'

'Because you left me alone.'

'Shush.'

'You left it all to me. To save Da and feed everyone and, and ...' His body shook with grief.

'You weep like a girl,' said Judoc loudly, for the others to hear. Then, in a whisper: 'Oh brother. Little calf. You should have stayed at home.'

Andagin felt the stranger's gaze on him. 'Is he a man of art?'

'You must not ask questions.'

'Judoc, they are outlaws, it is a crime to shelter them.'

'They are bastard laws that say so.'

'Why are your faces painted?'

'You remember I used to tell you about the man I met on the heath. When I was little. Before the sanctuary fell. He spoke to me, remember?'

'To ask the way.'

'I told him. And when I turned to watch there was no man but a raven flying above the heather. They have the gift of changing shape. They are close to the gods. They can see into the time of ancestors and into the times to come.'

'They did not see their own destruction.'

Judoc's face closed. It was worse, for Andagin, than the putting on of the hood. 'I have kept you from a beating, or worse, because you are of my blood and I am trusted. But all I can do for you now is to keep you from injury. He has decided that you must stay. At least until this work is done. You might betray us.'

'How can I betray you?'

Judoc unfolded out of his crouch, and the world felt colder without him close. Andagin whimpered: 'I can barely feel my hands.'

'Stop fighting then. Sit and be quiet and ask no questions.'

'You are needed at home.'

'This,' said Judoc, 'this is home.' He lifted the hood.

'At least spare me that!'

It hung, an obscene thing, beside his brother's thigh. 'One word from you and he will put it on.'

'He?'

'Someone has to watch you.'

'Do not leave me alone with him.'

The tears scalded Andagin's cheeks. His brother walked to the man of art and spoke with him briefly. The man frowned, glanced at Andagin, gave a curt nod.

The man stood up, with difficulty from his blasted leg, and the young friends surrounded him. From his pouch he produced small green offerings. Andagin peered and squinted: they were brooches made of mistletoe. The man limped among the boys, issuing each with a brooch. On

four bowed heads he laid his hands and spoke first to the
earth and then to heaven. Aesu and Lugh trembled. He
spoke words to them that Andagin could not hear, until
the weight of fear appeared to lift from their bodies.

The man of art bent down to the ground, near the shivering flanks of his wolfhound. When he righted himself,
his hands were laden. To each of the young men he
returned his belongings.

To Aesu and Lugh, their slings and oak clubs.

To Barocunas, a sword of iron and a spear of ash.

To Judoc, a quiver and the bow he hunted with.

The stranger bent into the bracken and raised aloft a
strange object, holding it parallel to his body so that
Andagin could not see it until it had been entrusted to his
brother.

Judoc held the instrument aloft. The others admired it,
staring in wonder at the staff of bronze with its curved tail
and, grafted to its tip, the gaping head of a boar.

The man of art carried from hand to hand what resem-
bled a gourd. The young men drank from it and fought an
impulse to gag at the contents. Each swallowed his
mouthful.

It was fully day, the sun clouded, a crabbed winter fruit.

The young men whooped and twitched and clapped one
another on the back. The man of art lifted his arms and
cast a net of words over them.

Andagin watched his brother and kinsmen run headlong out of the grove.

5

No Man's Land

She likes to approach the heath along the bridle path, to emerge as from a tunnel of trees into the expanse of winter grass. At her feet the footpath is a puzzle of sunlight, branches rummaging the pieces. The breeze smells of dead bracken and sand and gorse flowers.

The trees fall away. Bobbie enters the heath.

The sky has clouded over, so that she casts only the stain of a shadow, a shadow's ghost. She can imagine, for a moment, that she is alone in the world.

She follows the bridle path, though it is tempting to take one of the gullies carved by dirt-bikes. She can understand the allure of cutting your own path. Who wants to follow a straight official route when everything in nature loops and circles?

The air is sweet with the coconut scent of gorse flowers. She searches for and selects two large flints – chaps them together. That eggy smell, like gunpowder. She chaps them again and orange sparks tickle her skin. She lifts the flints to her lips. They are hot.

On the brow of the hill, under fizzing power lines, she gazes out across the Thames Valley. In some weathers it's possible to see as far as Canary Wharf, but today the air is smudged, a low bruise of particulates, and she can only just make out a conurbation, the arch of the new Wembley, the blocks and cubes of the City half dissolved and ghost-like on the horizon. London – the Great Wen as her grand-father called it, gnawing into England's flesh.

A green woodpecker flashes out of cover. Bobbie watches it flicker – wingbeat, dip, wingbeat, dip – into the wood. Coal tits mutter in a mist of birches, and looking for the birds her eyes are drawn to the concrete bunker atop the slope. Her grandfather explained the bunker to her. He called it a blockhouse. The Germans had built hundreds of these on the French coast, long ago during the war, and Allied soldiers trained right here to attack and neutralise them. Inside the bunker there are plastic bottles and crisp packets; she knows better than to investigate. Instead, she contemplates the heath, the dark treeline, and the iron man of her father's childhood, the telecommunications tower.

When he was a boy, her father believed that it was equipped with an early warning system. In case of a nuclear missile attack from the Soviet Union, he and Grannie and Grandpa would have had three minutes to get under the stairs and cover their heads with blankets. Would that have helped? Of course not – you cannot prepare for the end of the world. Her father doesn't dwell on nuclear weapons now. That was her grandmother's cause, that sent her to the Women's Peace Camp at Greenham Common and on marches to the Atomic Weapons Establishment at Aldermaston. No, what keeps her father awake, online until the early hours, is news from the biosphere, of resource depletion and global warming. It's the weather that fright-ens him, that frightens Bobbie through him and for him.

She turns her back on the rough concrete of the bunker and extracts the water bottle from her rucksack. In the haste of her thirst she knocks her teeth on the metal rim. She drinks, staring round the bottle at pine saplings growing through the heather. When she has stowed the bottle, she takes a few steps forward, bends at the waist and uproots two of them.

Dad's habit, it used to infuriate her mother.

'I don't know why you bother,' she said the last time they were together.; the week of Grandpa's funeral. 'Let the trees grow back if that's what they want to do.'

Her father huffed and strained against the taproots. 'They're the wrong kind of tree.'

'Can't we just go for a walk? You stopping every few metres to uproot trees, it's tedious.'

'Go on, I'll catch up with you.'

'There'll be more saplings further on. You'll never stop now you've started.' Mum and Bobbie watched him tearing up the upstarts. 'Richard!'

'What?'

'Left alone, the heath would revert to woodland. Who are you to stand in the way?'

'Left alone, everything reverts. Should we let the hill fort go under? Or the Devil's Highway?' This heralded a lecture about local distinctiveness and the significance of place. Bobbie could see the effect it was having on her mother. 'It's important to be rooted.'

'Rooted, yes, but you are stuck.'

Bobbie stalks along the sandy path, murdering young pines. For the good of the land. For her own satisfaction. She sets her teeth against the resistance of a sapling. Her hands are tacky with resin and sharp crystals of pain twist in her lower back. The meagre soil begins to warp and fracture, the taproot snaps and she stumbles backwards, the miniature pine trembling in her fist.

Her mother should have understood. She should have

cut him some slack. He was grieving, wasn't he? However difficult they all found Grandpa, he was still his father. Bobbie feels cold to imagine the same loss in her life. Her dear dad. She thinks of him searching the web at night, in Grandpa's study, the hours he spends liaising with – or is it pestering? – the forestry ranger and the MoD who patrol the heath and woods. One thing's for certain, he can't be getting any work done. It's almost a good thing her mother's not around to see it.

Bobbie calculates: four days since she last Skyped from Darfur. Her face flickering in a digital mist. Even when the picture froze, that calm-and-understanding voice droned on.

'You look after your dad, Roberta. He's an impossible man but we love him, don't we?'

'Oh yeah, you love him so much.'

'It's possible to love someone and not be able to live with them.'

'How's bloody Africa?'

'Darling. I am coming back. And when I do, when my posting is over, I won't go into the field for a long time, because you deserve to have me at home.'

'Which home? Ours in Oxford, or some shitty flat in London?'

'Home is where we are. We make it by being together.'

Bobbie wheezes with the effort of pulling up a sapling. She uproots its green star and straightens to contemplate what she has done. Forty or fifty grubbed up – thousands remain. She tosses the tree to break down slowly in the heather.

If he had a mission at his sister's, he flunked it. Here he is back on his tod, tramping across the heath, for lunch a

slice of white bread that sticks like gum to the back of his
teeth so he has to scrape it off with his fingernail. What's
he going to do with this day he's lumbered with? Lope
back to the vicarage and veg out in front of property
shows. Have a boredom wank in the lavender-scented
bathroom. His mind creeps to the sachet of resin under his
bed. He will skin up and lie back and let the skunk slap
him on the head till he's pinned down under it. Better than
brooding on that cunt Stu. He wanted Aitch out from the
moment he moved in. Aitch wasn't exactly good for much.
Up half the night, stubbing his toes in the dark and cursing. Playing shoot-em-ups on Barry's Xbox. Relying on
spliffs to get some kip and stinking out the flat so Bekah
was in his face when he stumbled to the kitchen at lunch-
time. He remembers the whispered lobbying – did Stu even
care that he could hear them? – behind closed doors. 'He's
gotta go, Bekah. We have responsibilities …' And Aitch
was stupid enough to hand him the ammo. Leaving cigarette burns in the sofa that time he fell asleep in front of
Red Hot TV. It was still on, volume down, when his niece
came into the room to play. Stu's rage, Bekah's look of
betrayal – they burnt him up. So he went off to sleep on
Donnie's couch in his pokey flat in Camberley, till Donnie
chucked him out for waking him up with his screaming.

He watches his step, down the very gullies that he
carved into the sand with his biking mates. He wouldn't
mind a ride, like in the old days, that engine throbbing
beneath him. Half a click away, a couple of lads are chuck-
ing stones at one another for laughs. Aitch recognises his
nephew Barry and that dickhead mate of his. He hails
them but they don't hear, or pretend not to.

Jog on, Aitch – the lad's ashamed of his homeless uncle.
When he signed up, he told Barry he'd be in the army for
twenty-two years. That's longer than a Roman legionary!

But he only served four. And now he's back where he started, or further back, living off the charity of a vicar who found him dossing in the porch of her church.

The Rev's all right. She's not stuffy like he'd imagined vicars. But then he's never had a reason to dislike them. The padre was sound, he'd seen the good in Aitch, in all of them. Reckoned if there was sin in war, it belonged to the politicians. But then he wasn't there, the day after Gobby and Chris – in the orchard.

Aitch is back in the woods. The canopy of new leaves closes over him. There's a smell of dry earth and something rotten.

He can always tell Rachel that Bekah was out. Doctor's appointment. Not that she'd interrogate him. There was only the once, that initial 'chat' about intoxicants in the vicarage. He told her not to worry about booze, his dad was a pisshead who fucked his liver, but the weed helps him to sleep.

'I'm not addicted,' he said.

'It's habitual.'

'Yeah, well, we all got our little habits.'

'Oh, for me it's Maltesers and boxsets. All the same, I am answerable to higher authorities, so no getting stoned on the premises, OK?'

He could have told her a thing or two about addiction. Coming out of the army is like coming off drugs, no one can really help you through it. The buzz of fighting – like nothing a civilian's ever experienced. And you come back home and no one has the faintest clue, and you're going cold turkey down the pub or in the bookie's or just lying on your back in bed and this feeling, which is mostly nothing, will last the rest of your fucking life. Some days he can't even remember why they were out there. Not for the Afghans. Not for Queen and Country. He fought for his mates, so he wouldn't be the one who let them down. Only here he's got no mates. Brewster's still in uniform. Dan fucked off to Australia to shear sheep. Rolfie slotted himself with his father's hunting rifle. It's just Aitch on his own and the knowledge he sleeps with under his pillow. He's an evil cunt and nothing the Rev says can change that. His heart will grow colder, it will darken till it's nothing but a black stone in his chest. And some days, the worst days, that doesn't even sound too bad.

She is waiting for them at the barrier to the Poors, her arms folded over her chest to show them she isn't impressed by anything they say or do. Darren and Barry. From the council estate. She met them three days ago when Darren was testing the suspension on his remote-controlled toy Jeep. Bobbie wouldn't use the word 'toy' in front of him but that's what it was, and they for all their swagger are children like her. Someone to hang out with, her secret friends, even if they do call her Robert and make fun of her accent and her reluctance to smoke.

They greet her sullenly – Barry with his crewcut and ugly black scabs, never explained, on both elbows, Darren whose voice has already broken, who stares at her when he thinks she doesn't notice.

'About time,' says Darren.

'What? I was here before you.' She sees Barry's top lip part from his teeth in what may be a grin or a response to the sun.

'Guess what we've found,' says Darren.

'What?'

'D'you wanna see?' asks Barry.

'It's not your willies, is it? Have you found those at last?'

Barry reddens but Darren snickers: 'You're on fire, Robert.'

'Rober–*ta*.'

'What kind of name is that, anyway?'

Darren gives his friend a shove. 'What kind of a name is Barry, Barry?' He peers at her from under his dark, tousled fringe. The way he swaps sides excites her. Confuses her too. 'Why don't you come and see,' he says.

The boys duck under the metal pole of the barrier and Bobbie follows. An orange-tip butterfly tumbles up from the warm gravel. Darren and Barry are running, looking across their shoulders to check that she's coming. Deliberately she keeps to a walk. Let them skip ahead like billy goats.

The boys hurry into the pines on the edge of Barossa Common, and for an instant she wonders if she should follow them. Her father would blow a fuse if he knew. But what is there to know? Why shouldn't she have friends and do as she pleases?

The air under the pines is close and smells of resin. The boys are looking at something. Heaped against the flank of a tree stands a mound of soil and pine needles. The surface of the heap stirs minutely – a simmering ferment. The boys are silent, and leaning closer Bobbie hears a noise from the hill like soft rain. These are wood ants, she wants to say. There are workers and soldiers, a complex society, almost one being. The soldier ants squirt formic acid – lower a stick in there and it will come out smelling like vinegar.

'You got it?' Darren asks.

'Nicked it off my stepdad,' says Barry.

One of the soldier ants is clambering up Bobbie's shoe. She doesn't lean down to remove it because Barry is holding a small yellow bottle. The bottle has a long plastic nozzle. He hands it to Darren. Darren shakes the bottle and picks off the miniature cap. He takes a sniff at the contents. 'Phwoar!' He wafts the open nozzle in front of Barry's face – 'Thirsty?' – then waves it at Bobbie. 'How 'bout you?'

'No,' says Bobbie.

'Just a sip. Might not kill you.'

Darren reaches into his right-hand trouser pocket. He extracts his fist, shakes it and it rattles.

The soldier ant has reached the bare skin of Bobbie's ankle.

'You wanna do it?'

'No!'

'We'll let you,' says Barry, 'if you're not scared.'

'I'm not.'

'Go on then.' Darren is squinting at her as if there's grit in his eye. He shakes the box and the matches chatter.

'She's a pussy,' says Barry.

'Shut up, dickhead,' says Darren.

Bobbie looks down. The soldier ant has clamped its jaws about her skin – a pinprick of fire.

Darren points the yellow bottle at the anthill, like someone trying to work a remote control with low batteries. He squeezes the bottle and a fine jet spurts out. Bobbie sees the ants going about their business under this bitter rain. The bottle gasps and wheezes. Darren gives it a testing shake and throws it at Barry. 'Your stepdad won't mind,' he says.

'You don't know him.'

The pain from the ant makes Bobbie's mouth water. She crumbles and smacks at it. Kill, kill!

Darren has lit a match and is sheltering it with his hand as he lowers it over the anthill. A blue rill races away from the match, and *whump*, a dome of flame covers the heap.

Darren and Barry whoop and squirm like little boys who need the loo.

'It went up like a fuckin' bomfire!'

The anthill burns as fast and as hot as gorse. Bobbie realises that Darren is looking at her. She sees his slanting grin and the unconscious gyration of his hips. 'That fire will spread,' she says. 'The ground's too dry.'

Barry kicks at the nest and vapour sallies from its choking tunnels.

'We'll have the fire brigade after us. Darren, I'm serious!'

He looks at her. 'All right,' he says, 'we'll have to put it out.' She sees him reach for his flies and unzip them. He extracts a pale tuber and grips it with his fingers.

She turns her head as Darren pisses into the ant heap. 'You gonna help me?' he says when Barry sniggers, and now both boys have their backs turned, their shoulders hunched.

Bobbie wants to run. She hates them. There's a smell of ammonia and the nest is still smouldering. Darren and Barry beat it with sticks and try to smother it with pine needles kicked up from the ground. 'Could do with more piss,' shouts Barry, and both of them laugh.

'Fuck off,' she says, and she walks away. Barry calls after her derisively, and though she half hopes Darren might chase her into the open, she is also relieved when she gets to the Poors Allotment without company. She moves fast, her legs taut and burning under the sun, down the hill, past the blockhouse with its obscene graffiti. The slope and her momentum see her running, racing even, down the bridle path towards the trees. She hears the cooing of woodpigeons. *Who did it, not me. Who did it, not me.* A plump sound that belongs to summer – falling asleep on the old recliner under the oaks in her grandfather's garden.

6

The Heave

Too hot the day we go foragin on the heave in the shade of a woody hill. Becca Rona dig for sand crickets, Nathin hold the guidin stick bash a lizard an roast it on a pile of flints. Efia look thru the stores, pack after pack. She pass round the plasters then the jercans. Enuf water for a nuther day maybe two if we go slow after nightfall.

Samewhile Malk Aban scout the country. Open sand an thorn an furze. Dips here an there with low pines cracklin in the heat. North theres Brag Nell, a fat sted tho we know best avoid it. Malk grip his sharpstick lookin left an right but Aban walk easy, chappin two stones together for the tickly orange spark an the rotty egg smell. Thru dry trees they come on a stone track. An old path of flint an dead branches. Trees creakin over it, lots blown down but still the ways clear. A stretch of it leadin west like the story say.

Davys Way, say Malk.

Must be, say Aban.

Some hunnerd yards they follow the track, stoopin under tree trunks, clamberin over where stoopins impossible, till they know it go on for real. Dead roads story spoke far back as Stains an Winser. How once on a time a clever bloke call Davy come this way cross the stony desert an find a little boy weepin on a rock. Boo woo, say the little boy an Davy say, Wassup little boy, dont waste all that water in this desert so dry. Boy look up at Davy, see his pointy tail an say, Im cryin cos my mum an dad sent me out to pick rambles an now I cant find my way home. So Davy think on this some then say, Wheres yer mum an dad, an the little boy say, Where the sun set come nightfall. Sun set westway, say Davy, but listen we is east where the sun rise an wests far away but dont cry cos Davy can help you. Help me, say the little boy, an what for? What for, nuthin you aint usin just yer soul little boy when yer old an croakit then Davy come an take it. Far far off, say Davy, so far an I bet you cant even think on it. Home, say Davy. Homes waitin for you, mum an dads callin for you. What you say eh? So the little boy think, he cant see his soul nor smell it, where is it an all? So rightyer, he say, an they shake on it an like an earthquake the ground shake an cross the wastes before em a road appear straight like a spear. Up it crack an there it go from where the sun rise to where the sun set. Now run home little boy, say Davy, an the little boy run, he skip an leap for joy, mum an dad they will be glad, an he run home not once lookin back to see Davy wavin, an home he run an its hugs an kisses an safer sound till years pass, long happy years an the boy grow big an old like no time passin an hes lyin on his deathbed with his kiddies all round him an knock knock he hear, knock knock tho no one else can hear it an Davys back lookin like the day long ago an Wassup, say Davy, an he snatch him up an wrap him in his pointy tail an long a black an fiery road he take him to a hotter place an a lonesum an hes down there still cryin woe under the sharp tooth an claw of Davy.

Malk Aban look long the road. Dont like it, say Malk. Like someones watchin us.

Out here, say Aban, whod that be?

Dunno. Just dont feel right.

Least we know the way it go. No steds nor juntamen on it.

Lets go.

Fastest they can they push thru scrub. The brush so loud the carders shush an hoppers skit an scatter at they feet. No way now but forwards, so coverin faces with keffiyas Malk Aban crash on till trees fall back an thorns part an a mound, a great hump of earth, stand before em. A hill of sand an black stumps an ash where fires bin playin.

Malk kick up a sign paint on wood but he cant read the words nor can Aban. They wonder bout the hill. Signs of campment here an there. Stone circles from cookin fires. Pieces of flint knap for cuttin. A bucket with nuthin in it but holes.

Look say Malk an Aban follow his point to arrowheads an woodshafts here an there. Signs of fightin, tho from when who can say.

Cross country eh, say Malk, an gob the dust.

Here, say Aban, an he clamber down the hills rampart. Two shelves of earth an a dell below. Shelter from view down crumbly ribs of earth.

Deep under the hill a coverin of grass like a den for kids to play in. A special hidey place no grownups know. Lie down an all sight of yous gone. Like fallin under a wave of seed.

Lyin face to face in the grass Malk Aban touch. Good for you mate?

West Cunnys no closer.

We sleep here. Group maybe. Build us up for the push west.

Long Davys Way?

If all gree.

Just for one night, say Malk. Famines comin an war. Heave cant keep us.

Two nights, say Aban, an back they go to fetch the others.

Suns lower, not stabbin so hard when Malk Aban get back. Abans got a flint in his fist he find on the way. It catch his eye cos of its red colour an turnin it over he like the way it fit in his palm. Its shape like a womans body. Hes rollin it in his fingers nabberin to Malk when Malk click him to shush.

Look. With Becca Rona. Some bloke.

Wheres Nathin, say Aban.

Malk, eyes burnin, turn over his sharpstick but Aban say, Easy. Hes got no weapon an girls dont look fraid.

Could be slavers scout or bounty man.

Well an if so hes found us. Best show him whos boss.

So movin out open they walk an Aban shout, Sup, an all heads turn, the new blokes also. Scrawny like an old chook. Rags about him. Arms like tar ropes, the muscles showin an no inch of fat. Eyes big an fraid. A famish scaredy crow.

Becca Rona up an say, Hes a friend.

To who, say Malk.

To us, say Efia. Hes lost.

Wheres Nathin?

Huntin.

With the guidin stick?

We dint need guidin, say Efia, just waitin for you.

Aban look to her case these words only an dangers ready to come hollerin thru the trees. But he find no bad in her face an put a hand on Malks shoulder tho Malk shrug it off an go to the new bloke an stand in his face sayin, Whos this then whos this?

Salam, say new bloke.

Malk say, Im the leader on this group an ousters aint welcome.

This one is, say Efia. His names Dowd.

The stranger rest a palm on his chest.

Wheres he from, say Malk.

Nathin find him. Just walkin, say Rona. All tire an thirsty so we give him water.

He find his own, say Malk. Dont go wastin.

Please. You have no reason to fear me.

Strange this Dowds way of speakin. A young bloke but Aban Malk know oldsters in the Wen speak much the same way. Sort of like old writin would speak if it could.

Well, say Malk, an now you drink other folks water you best be off aint you.

Dowd show his teeth but its a smile like he aint understandin. Dowds body shimmer like a bloke seen in heat only close up an his eyes flicker into they sockets an down he tumble. Rona Becca Efia Aban close bout him but Malk standin say, Hes sick. Malair got him or teebee.

Not Malair, say Efia. Just hunger. An you aint our leader Malk. Nors anyone.

Nathin find the group just so, Malk standin ragin with his sharpstick while others bend over the new bloke. Malk see Nathin an shout, You! Dont fuck off takin the guidin stick with you.

I bin huntin.

For squirrels, say Malk, an its true all Nathins got is one squirrel corse. Nathin look down at his catch an then at the group. Is he dead, he say.

Good as, say Malk. Best leave him.

No, say Efia.

Nuther gob to fill in this shithole? Weightin us down an we gotta get to West Cunny.

Hes scapin like us, say Efia. Just like us Malk.

Sez you, say Malk. Could be a spy. Thick with hoofers or juntamen or worse.

Malk, say Rona an shes soft an calm. Hes legit. Look. From the snorin body she pull back rags to show a thistle of scars on Dowds back. Fuck say Aban. The fat welts like wormcasts in mud. All branchin crisscross like spores under the skin. Then Becca Rona turn him over an on his right arm theres an ouster brand.

Malk stare long at the scars. What if hes sick, he say.

Tired an hungry is all, say Rona.

Nathin look set to speak but Malks eyes shush him. So Becca speak Nathins thinks for him. One more set of arms an legs innit. Safety in numbers. With Lan gone –

Don't, say Malk. But Efia pick up her thinks an say, Lans gone an heres a new friend. What you reckon Aban?

Aban feel her look on his face. Efias foot reach cross the sand an kick him on the shin till he say, True. True mate. Nuther bloke make the group stronger an safer.

Nathin, say Malk. Any thinks?

Nathin look at the guidin stick like its a poison snake he want to drop. Dunno, he say.

Becca Rona?

Keep him, say Rona.

Keep him, say Becca.

So all gree tho Malk scowl an go sit elseway till Dowd croak or wake up.

Listen, say Efia to Aban. Malks gettin big for his boots. He cant call his self leader. Group dont have no leader just the group an alls level.

Malk dont mean nuthin by it.

Sez you Aban. Cos you mates.

Aban feel a heaviness in his chest. He think back to the nip of Efias toe on his skin. Theres a campment, he say.

Eh?

We find one. On our recky. Safe place to sleep.

Hes comin back look.

Sure enuf Dowd come round an stare like he cant remember. Easy, say Efia.

Please!

Dont be fraid.

No!

This Aban hes with us. You stay an all. Eat an drink then off we go. Wheres Malk?

Aban look up the woody hill where Malks sittin on a tree stump starin cross the land to the Wen. Theres a road, say Aban. It ul take us where we goin.

Any stedders on this road, say Rona.

No. Dead road really. Davys Way.

Wind pick up harsh from south an tug at our clothes like it want to steal em. White sand swarm at our legs, each grain takin a bite. Malk look at Dowd an say, Hes slowin us, but Efia give Dowd a shoulder an tell Aban to help. So we get slow to Davys Way an now scrub oaks shelter us from the stingin wind. No nabberin till Malk say, Heres the place an out the woods we come to the hill. Efia find the rotty sign with its black letters an read out the words, Old Fort.

Theres more writing, say Dowd heavin for breath. Under the paint.

Becca look all round say, This it? More dust an ole fires? Wheres the campment?

Ah, say Aban.

Malk Rona Becca Nathin Efia Dowd follow Aban down Old Forts flank. Whoop of the wind cease an the sand stop bitin. Alls quiet down here, the grass green an tall enuf for sleepin under. Hide here, the hill one way an thorns the other.

What yer reckon, say Aban grinnin at Efia. For answer she stretch an lie down. Bone tired but safe.

For supper only pears found on the roadside. Rona Becca take out blades, scrape away the needles, wipe the sharpness off a stone. Efia take a pear to the boy. He swallow some of the pip flesh then turn his head an puke it up. Aban watch Efia move her hand on the boys back. When she try to give him more he take it from her.

Dont waste, say Aban. Boy ul eat when hes ready.

Nightfall rouse us. Dowd most of all. Like hes tryin to make him real for the group he start to speak. Clever words in the old time way like Malk Aban use to hear when they slaves under Feo.

I will tell you, say Dowd, how I came to be here. Why I am running and what from.

Dowd tell the group how he born in a dust storm. Folk all owners like folk before em. Treat slaves in kind ways tho. Malk gob at these words. Malk the scaped slave. Efia also angry till she think on the welts on Dowds back an the ouster brand on his arm.

Life in my village was hard, say Dowd because of the Dry. Still we might have stayed. But the fighting caught up with us.

A nipper no more, his sted get took by looters. He recall the blades hackin. Blood dryin in the earth. Not even dogs left to lick it. Slaves dead, sisters stole, he sail with his folks cross the stinkwater. Thirst carry off his ma, give her to the crabs an jellies. Pa an Dowd make it ashore with thousand other ousters all lookin for life, a patch of ground, a scrap of bread. Dowd an Pa stuck in cages pendin a rulin. One day it come, they flesh burn, the air full of screams an scorchin smell.

They branded us, say Dowd, then took us to a waiting place. An island in the river.

Two miles long an one half wide of salt flats an marshy woods. Water no good for drinkin, only what the junta keep in tanks under armed guard. To save his pa Dowd look for bread. First handout from a barge an many trod to death. Dowd give up his shirt an shoes for a loaf.

Why they take you ousters there? What for, say Becca.

They told us we would be moved to a special village. That is why we had no tools to make things. No ovens or grain. But we never came off the island. They left us there to die.

Dowd tell us bout the island. How folk everyway hungry an nuthin to eat but rotty loaves pile up out of reach an juntamen guardin em. Sun scorchin, rain peltin, some rig shelters with branches an palm fronds. Sickos in rows all muck an lice. An every way the stink of squits an gobs runnin black with gumdrip. Old Malair sit down with folk then. Lay his cold hand on em, huff his hot breath in they throats. Parents holding they kiddies gone rigger cos Malair got em in his teeth.

What, say Malk. An you just sit there takin it?

Some people tried to escape. The juntamen killed them. Also locals to save their crops.

An yer pa? This Efia say an Aban look cos her eyes gone soft, she lean like shes gonna touch Dowd.

I watched him die. Just gave up. Saying Mas name and my sisters.

He leave you, say Malk.

Yes.

Then you well rid, say Malk. But Dowd seem not to hear or else he make like he dont.

About a month after they put us on the island the hunting started. Men were very hungry. For punishment the junta burned our rations in front of us.

You mean, say Becca, blokes eat other blokes?

I had to hide in ditches at night hoping they would not find me. Then one day a man came to me. He gave me fish to eat. Bad fish all rotted but I wanted to live. His name was Ned. He planned to leave the island with two men strong like him.

Strong how, say Malk, if an you all starvin?

Up and off –

How they stay fit on weeds an rotty fish?

Dowd look at his ankles. Up and off, he say, before day and no one to stop us.

Most on the island just ghosts now or stickmen. Bird beaks for mouths. Heron legs too thin to stand. But Ned an the two blokes still strong an they slip into the water with Dowd on a raft of branches. In salt marsh they find sunfire plant an eat it. Also seabeet an snaily crits. Ned call em winkers cos you wink em out with a pin. Fact the shells so weak you can break em with finger an thumb. Pick off specks eat the meat. Like salty snot. Still it keep em movin.

That first night, say Dowd, we hid in a ruin. The two men looked away but Ned was kind and gave me food.

What food, say Malk.

Ned was a soldier before he was trafficked. Sometimes he shouted in the dark. The other men woke him. His dreams were bad.

What happen, say Becca, when you get to the Wen?

Ah. Dowd breathe in like hot broths on his lips. The Wen, he say. We did not get there.

Why?

The two men wanted to go north. Up the midlands where the juntas not so strong.

An Ned?

Ned wanted the Wen but he was one and they were two.

So you follow.

Yes.

Cross marsh an thru bush. Hidin in grassland stealin food but never enuf cos the two blokes want to go faster an faster. They put they heads together at night. In hollows or shells of manshuns they whisper an Ned look Dowd in the eye. But Neds eyes say nuthin to Dowd, like fish eyes they share no thinks.

We got hungry, say Dowd. Very hungry. And when we had walked for days I woke up with Neds hand on my mouth. At first I was scared but then in his face I saw he was the scared one. Dowd, he said, you must go. I said, Why and where and he said, You are in danger. Take this food take this water and run. But I could not move so he pushed me saying, We are bad men. We take you with us off the island for a goat.

Nathin snort an laugh. A goat!

Its what he said.

Like for milk!

For meat.

Nathin shush at that.

When they took me off the island it was not kindness. I was food that carried itself and stayed fresh. When Ned told me this I said I did not believe him. But I did believe. When the two men whispered together it was about me. Ned said they were going to do it very soon and, Go now, he said, go and forgive me.

So you run, say Efia.

I ran. Fast as my legs could go. For two days until other men found me. Tradesmen from the north. They caught me sleeping and I was taken. That is how I came to be traded and sent as a prentice to Brag Nell.

Prentice, say Malk, risin an standin bove Dowd his teeth showin. Slave you mean just like the rest of us.

I was a slave, say Dowd. But I got away and now I am free.

No ones free, say Malk, just on a longer chain is all. An he kick up dust an turn away. Others sit with Dowd soakin up his story whiles Malk go up the bank of Old Fort an start settin dewcloths for the nightspit. Dowd look up to him, his eyes shinin, teeth stark in moonlight. Efia look at the scar, a welt like a pop belly nub on the boys arm. His ouster patch. His cross-the-water mark. Aban too have a scar, a brand from the slaver that hold him. Dowd talk an Efia put her finger on the lump on Abans neck. The Slave Cross. He catch her fingers, hold em a bit then put em gentle down. She look at him. Thinkin on her life an now the road, the group, this skinny dark ouster crouchin in the grass tellin his story.

All done an the group set down to sleep. Aban Efia Nathin Becca Rona like one tangle of limbs an Dowd outsight watchin. See Malk come down after dark an try a smile but Malk keep his lips tight an squat next the group lookin at the stars.

What were you doing, say Dowd. Up there?

Malk say nuthin but turn his sharpstick.

There used to be a village.

Where?

Here, say Dowd. Long ago.

In the Fast Time?

Before.

Malk chew on this. Who ever think on *before* before? Fast Times before an past that who can say. Malk shrug like to shift sumthin off his back.

Sez you, he say. Just a hill to me. No before bout it just mud an sand.

Dowd nod. Perhaps you are right.

Right enuf an lead this lot. Malk rush thru grass to Dowd till hes breathin in his face. Right enuf an you play ball cos I aint blind to spies nor blokes as dont have good at heart.

You have no reason to fear me.

Well lets see. For now one fast move whiles we sleep an yer blood ul answer for it.

I too will sleep.

An thats all you do. Cos I got one plan an one plan only thats get us all to safety.

Dowd nod an show his palms.

Rightyer?

Good night, say Dowd.

Good night an all. Ouster scum.

7

Blueface

The dullness, the stink and tedium of winter quarters lay far behind them. Riding occupied all of their senses.

Marcus enjoyed the lash of the cold: it scoured his face, while the wind whooped and rising clods of ice spangled the air. It was the privilege of horsemanship to have such power at his command. The aches and fevers of confinement fell away. Surely the other riders felt it? He half expected to hear them shout for joy.

After many miles of open heath and pasture, the land thickened into scrub oak and gorse. The latter, resurgent, grew almost to the road. It was abundant where their mission ended.

'Here it is,' said Marcus.

Three kerb-stones had been dislodged and broken paving, like the sea where a wall is breached, had spilled through the gap, exposing the rough layer of gravel beneath. No flood had caused this – even supposing the land could produce one in such a freeze.

'Boar?'

The engineer looked admiringly at Lucius Agilis. 'Why not elephant while you're at it?' Celer dismounted, inelegantly, to commune with the damage.

Marcus watched the engineer. He disliked the expression on his face. 'Ought we to mount guard?'

'You're the cavalry officer, I leave that to you. But I can tell you this: if wild animals are to blame, they're uncommonly handy with picks and axes.' Celer bent, with a mutter of discomfort, as though his back were troublesome, and indicated the dents in the paving stones where they had been prised off the cement.

'Idle boys perhaps,' said Glyco, 'full of spunk and void of sense?'

Marcus dismounted. One hand on the bridle, he bolstered himself with the other above his kneecap and peered at the evidence.

Later, when he attempted to reconstruct what followed, he would recall no hint of movement in the gorse along the road. The profound quiet of snowfields, the scraping hooves of the horses: nothing more. Only Glyco speaking the name of his comrade and Lucius Agilis seemingly intent on picking something from his horse's nape.

Marcus had to pay his glance a second visit. Lucius Agilis had dwindled in his saddle. He slumped forward, his mouth slack and a look of brutishness in his eyes. Gods, he's having a stroke – and Celer was rushing to prop him up lest he break a limb in his fall.

The next arrow pierced the flank of Glyco's horse.

Glyco was thrown and writhing on the road. The horse screamed and stamped and Lucius was falling, a shaft in his back.

The air pulsed with a sound Marcus had never heard, though he knew it at once. The bellowing of a carnyx.

Marcus struggled to draw his sword. The engineer appeared to be pissing blood.

The heath itself rose up against them.

*

He was at sea, sickened by punishing swells. The world lurched and dipped. His stomach turned over.

He lay on the shore of wakefulness, weak with nausea and dread. Cries echoed in his mind. He remembered the hilt of a sword in his hand, saw it open a cleft of flesh.

Pain eddied about his skull like the note of a gong.

His left eye revealed a skein of light and green branches. His right eye would not open: a bloated fruit, it oozed gum over his fingers when he touched it. Hot, weeping pain followed, but harder to bear was the clarity of his knowledge – *I am their captive.*

He sat up, or tried to, for his legs and wrists were bound and a foot belonging to a powerful body pressed him back into a lattice of roots. Sickness welled up inside him: he vomited and tried to wriggle away from the reeking spatter. There was laughter, shallow and mirthless.

A wintry sky brimmed over the lip of a green bowl. He was in that bowl, unable to clamber out. He tried to speak, to issue orders for his release.

Someone replied in his own language. 'Worm,' the voice said. 'Horse soldier worm.'

Like a worm he contemplated the descending sole of a boot. It pressed into his cheek. He grimaced to keep his cry locked inside him.

The boot relented. Marcus waited, gradually lifting his face clear of the cold earth. He found he was able to shuffle into an awkward sitting position. Fearfully, he inspected his groin, his thighs, his belly. He was whole, and relief brought new light to his functioning eye.

He was in a clearing of evergreens. To judge from the light on the upper branches, the sun was at its zenith.

Men stood in a knot about a prone body. He could not make out much of the injured man. The brute who had called him worm watched him from a distance.

Where was his company? He searched for them among the trees.

Glyco was bound by a rope about his neck to a stake in the ground. His face was a mask of blood, the eyes within it stark and terrible. Marcus tried with the heat of his one eye to hail them. The Sicilian returned his gaze.

– Are you hurt?

– What does it look like? You?

Marcus tried to shrug but a yoke of pain forced his shoulders down. What about Celer? Lucius?

Glyco stared at him.

Marcus bowed his head. He tried to piece together the fragments of what had befallen them. Doing so muted the taunting voice, very like that of his father, which called him a failure, a disgrace to the standard, killer of his own men.

Think.

The arrow in Lucius Agilis.

The screaming horse.

He saw the enemy rushing at them, their howling faces red and blue. His sword sang free; a spear and clubs jabbed at his swinging blade. He saw Glyco, a whirlwind, crashing into the throng, Celer kneeling in a puddle of blood. A fury had possessed his sword and dragged itself through the skin and bone of a painted face. His foe went down, Glyco was raging, and Marcus realised that these were not warriors but boys, and that outnumbered as they were, he and the Sicilian – thank the gods for his crazed strength –

might yet survive this. Then his awareness of a flame-haired youth flourishing a sling, and the warning that sounded in his body, too late, to duck the stone that came and extinguished everything.

Marcus tried to get to his knees but the watchful brute gave a bellow. In a moment the others were about him: the savages of his childhood nightmares, their chests and arms and faces painted. Mere boys, yet strong and angry enough to hurt him. He was powerless to defend himself against their kicks and punches and the spit that foamed on his face and sheltering arms.

A cry like the beginning of a song enchanted the mob. Their blows and insults ceased. He saw the youths part before a man of middle years: one not painted like them, his hair free of stiffening lime, for he had, with eyes like those, no need of a disguise to lend terror to his aspect.

Marcus knew at once where his fortunes lay.

He had never seen a druid in the flesh. Their island stronghold had been broken, their brotherhood forbidden. In Gaul they had long ago been absorbed into the peace. The physical fact of the man filled Marcus with awe, as if Pan himself had wandered into the grove.

'You,' the druid said, then spoke words that Marcus could not follow, though he knew they were not native.

'Let me go. Release me and the other. Or it will go heavily with you.' The painted faces loomed. So few of them: a kind of suicide. He had no faith in his tongue to attempt theirs, yet spoke for the relief of hearing his voice above the druid's incantations. 'This can achieve nothing,' he said. 'Only ruin for your people.'

He flinched, for the druid's hand was coming towards him. With wounding gentleness it caressed his cheek. 'Soon,' the man said, then stood and frayed another gap in the mob. It did not close immediately, and Marcus watched

him lope back to the injured figure on the ground. He
recognised the blond hair, now stiff with blood. It was the
young man he had cut down.

So he and Glyco were condemned. There would be
punishment, of course. Aulus Pomponius Capito would
not limit reprisals to the perpetrators. Probably he would
be glad of blood to spill, to relieve the winter's boredom.
But all would come too late for them.

The decurion bowed his head to pray. No prayers came.
He looked again at his ragtag captors. It was a surprise to
see a third captive propped against the trunk of a dying
yew. A young boy. Not in war gear. Watching him without
fear or hatred. A British child, uneasily seated, a bruise
ripening on his frozen cheek.

***

He asked himself what was the worst. Was it the cold, or
to have been bound like an animal by his own brother?
Was it watching the man of art take possession of the
grove, or the sight of those foreigners whose humiliation
could cost them everything? He turned his mind to the
question and concluded with something like relief – for it
brought clarity to his suffering – that the worst was Aesu's
breathing, guessing from the faces of Judoc and Lugh and
Barocunas that his life was spilling away, that a portal
had been opened through which death might claim them
all.

The man of art was kneeling beside Aesu. He held a
pouch of leather and from it he took something and placed
it in Aesu's mouth. He clamped both hands over Aesu's
face to prevent him spitting out what he was meant to
swallow. Andagin's kinsmen gathered to watch, and when
the man stood they parted to let him go.

After so much whispering, it was a shock to hear the man of art speak.

'Do not fear,' he said, 'for the life of your brother. I have sent him to a place where pain holds no sway. He has done good work. As have you all done good work, though it is yet unfinished. For no journey into danger is complete without a return. I mean a return to honour and the favour of our gods.'

The man of art hobbled from one youth to another, perching a hand on their necks and shoulders.

'Oh my boys. It does me good, it fills the deep dry well of my being with sweet waters to see you armed and right-eous. Thanks to you the war horn has sounded again in Ierne. Thanks to you our queen may rest a little, the ghosts in our strongholds feel in part avenged. Because of what you have done.

'And yet, and still, we have the test of a winter's dark ahead of us. For we may not light a fire against the cold, nor ask for shelter in the meanest hut. I ask your patience while the night runs its course. You must keep these men alive with furs and your own bodies if need be. At first light, when we take them to the pool, we will need them fit for sacrifice.

'When that time comes, do not let softness enter your hearts. Do not be led astray by compassion – for what tenderness is there in admitting the rape of your sister, the murder of your brother?'

Andagin's soul was lost to him. It belonged, while the man of art spoke, to those sonorous unfamiliar vowels, their gravel and smoke. Even the dog sat alert, its great head lifted, eyes fixed on its master.

'I have travelled in the places of the enemy. I have seen the diseases of his rule. So do not, my sons in vengeance, be womanish at the last. Remember the blow that felled

Aesu. Remember the shame of your fathers that you will not accept as your inheritance.

'For who amongst you chose humiliation? Who traded his freedom for this disgraceful peace?

'Old men. Old men who sit closest to the fire with the choice cuts before them. When they glance at you with their pale eyes, their paunches spreading, do they see elders of the future? No. They are too drunk to look. Too well fed on the flattery of their masters. They made a bargain before you were born and it has given them easy lives. But none of that ease awaits you. No thigh pieces for you – only the gizzard and gristle. No poet's song and the bedtime eyes of women. Only dishonour. Only shame.

'Once, the word *we* lived in our mouths and *I* was as a visiting stranger. We had our trackways and spirits that kept them. But spirits need the worship of use. Today the old ways close over and men cleave to the road, seeing it as a path to riches. Which of you has not a brother, a cousin or uncle who sacrifices to Mircurios? A god, not of the sacred places, not of the harvest or thunder of battle, but of *trade*. A god of haggling and purses.

'Oh, the enemy is cunning. He pays men to ply the sea between his language and ours. He recruits them into the army of occupation, setting father against son, uncle against nephew. The land itself he takes from us. Does he not fell our sacred groves and build his temples upon them? And are these temples not filled with blasphemies – their Divus Augustus who was but a man? Who can protect us from these gods that look like men and act like monsters? Who can walk the rage from his belly when the land is broken and cannot hold it?

'My sons, you will hear men in these parts call the Uprising a failure. They will point to lives lost but not to honour saved. Was it a failure that destroyed a legion?

Was it a failure that loosened the roots of their rule? Had Ierne in all her strength risen, we would have driven the occupiers back into the sea. It was not faith or the lack of it that did for us. It was the cowardice of your elders. A shame they mean to ram down your throats. And will you kneel like supplicants while this happens? Will you watch dark blood mix with the blood of your daughters?'

'No!' Lugh shouted. Barocunas shouted, and Judoc, as if they did not have a legion after them: 'No, no!'

'No, my boys. You are the pure crop of this land. Through you the gods will have their vengeance.

'I ask you to think now. Think how these men have deserved your hatred. How stonily they watch you on their patrols. How lustfully they look at your mothers, turn you over with their eyes, making you feel like strangers in your own land.

'Tomorrow you will be strangers no more. Tomorrow you will come into your rightful kingdom.

'Judoc, take this pouch of seeds. You will put them in the soldiers' mouths to please the Goddess. They will ripen when she wears her dress of summer.

'You, Barocunas, the ox of our company, take this noose. May you have the strength to use it.

'Brave Lugh, take this knife. Let the hand not falter that must draw forth its spirit.

'My sons, you have tonight to ready your souls. You will spend it fasting, and your fast will ask more of you than hunger, for you will be reminded many times of what took place this day. Memory will come at you like the hunting owl. You will want to shrink from its claws. You will try to block your ears to its shrieking.

'Perhaps, when the sun rises and we stand beside the waters, you will doubt the hand that holds the rope and the knife. Perhaps your fathers will appear to you as voices on the wind. They will speak with anger or honeyed tongues about peace and trade. And it will cost you dear to silence them. Nor will your efforts cease when the offering is made. For you will become hunted men. Like me you will be outlaws. Yet I make you this promise – that you will return. Not into the bosoms of your families. There can be no rest in the world as it is. The return I see is into glory. There, kisses will wash your feet and tears of welcome wipe the blood from your faces. The kisses and the tears will belong to those that went before us, the warriors that died for our honour, the ancient children of the tribe. The favourites of the gods whose defeat, tomorrow, you will begin to undo.'

8

No Man's Land

When he invites himself into her room to open the curtains, he is complaining already about the heat. 'Everyone else,' yawns Bobbie, 'seems to love it.'

Her father tells her breakfast is ready. This means that he has lined up the cereal packets. It's more effort than he made yesterday, when Bobbie returned from the woods to find him – in zip-off trousers, bush shirt and his ridiculous Akubra hat – getting ready to drive out again. Louts, he said, had been starting fires in Sandhurst. He went up on the Poors to check, leaving Bobbie alone to wander about the house and make her own lunch. When her father came back – in the evening – he wanted only to watch the news, followed by *Newsnight*, and then retired to Grandpa's study, while Bobbie got into bed and let the tears trickle into her ears.

After a silent breakfast, she helps her father load the dishwasher. 'I'm afraid you're going to hate me,' he says. 'I have to go out.'

'Again?'

'I'm meeting the solicitor. I also need to visit Grandpa's tenants.'

'What for?'

'You know very well Grannie wants to sell the shops now he's no longer here to manage them.'

'Can I come?'

'You'd be bored stiff. Anyway, haven't you got home-work to do?'

Fat chance. She isn't going to stay put like some tame little girl in a Victorian novel, half expecting and entirely fearing her grandfather's ghost. As soon as Dad has backed the Vauxhall out of the driveway, she repacks her ruck-sack. This time she takes the OS map and her grandfather's compass.

Up Surrey Hill, pressing north, she hikes for an hour until she reaches Star Point, then follows the Devil's Highway towards Caesar's Camp.

Four miles from the shopping centres of Bracknell, on a warm spring day, and not one visitor beside herself.

The hill of the fort is uninhabited – a low plateau of grass and bracken, heather and furze. She dangles her legs over the edge of what may have held ramparts, sipping water and gazing into the old beeches. Her father took part in a dig here in the summer before he went up to Cambridge. They didn't find much – potsherds, no bones on account of the acid soil, and only small piles of corro-sion left by metals. Nonetheless, working on the counter-scarp bank, they did reach a layer of ash and cover sand that suggested fire, some kind of violence.

Probably there was a siege – hill forts were always getting caught up in sieges. It must pretty much have been the point of them.

Yesterday, Bobbie thinks, the hill was as it is today, and the day before, and hundreds of days before that. But if the world were like a film and you could rewind it, it would be possible to make many places out of one place. And people would be dug out of their graves, their hair would colour on their heads, their skin tighten, their bodies turn supple and strong, they would dwindle into childhood, into their mothers' arms, they would die in the womb. And this would go back up the generations, while the trees turn gold and bare and green again, shrinking to seed, the world unspinning on time's axis. It's too much to contain – her poor brain reels. She, Bobbie Borowski, is only a child, yet sometimes it feels as if the world is looking to her for something, like an excavation but of more than bones.

Mum would know what to do with these thoughts. Shut them in the drawer marked *random junk*.

'You want to keep a lid on nostalgia ...' She said this before Christmas, when Dad was raging at the tree lights which were on the blink and no match for the actual candles his parents used when he was a boy. 'It made an old git of your grandpa. I'm sorry to say your father suffers from it too. He thinks everything good belongs to the past, but the past was horrid. Women had no rights. You could die of sepsis from a small infection. And there were no painkillers. Travel back in time with a box of Nurofen and you'd be worshipped as a god.'

Some god, who can't even keep her parents together. They are going to get a divorce, just as her grandparents did after Grannie upped sticks and went to live in an intentional community. She remembers, though she was little at the time, the shock of the separation, Grandpa red-eyed at the front door, a flag of shirt sticking out of his unfastened flies. Bobbie wishes her grandmother were on the scene, but her father always thinks up excuses for not travelling to Lincolnshire to see her.

She came to the funeral, of course, her face puffed and haggard, her hands trembling as she held the service booklet. At the reception she seemed distracted, as woolly as her knitwear. It would have been hurtful to ask her questions, and Bobbie made no mention of the conversation she'd overheard a few months before Grandpa's death.

It was late autumn – their last visit as a family – and the lanes were a slush of mud and leaves. Only the night before, Grandpa had broken his thumb. In a fall, Dad said. Under the influence, added Mum, who made sure to camp out in the kitchen for much of their stay. Bobbie was between her father and her grandfather in the sitting room. Grandpa had produced, on a filthy plate, a stale brick of fruitcake.

'Papcio,' said Dad, 'Mummy tells me you've been goading her.'

'Puh!'

'Well haven't you?'

'I cannot get to Switzerland on my own.'

'She's not going to take you to Switzerland.'

'It is not a slaughter house, Richie. They do it cleanly and without pain.'

'Bobbie, why don't you go and watch television?'

'The child can listen.'

'Go,' said Dad.

She went to the utility room and stared at the TV with the sound on low.

'I thought it was a sin,' said Dad on the other side of the door.

'I am going blind, my body is failing. Why is it a sin to end things on my terms?'

'You haven't the first idea how long you might live.'

'Now it is cold I should walk out and let the night take me.'

'I'd be the one to find your corpse.'

'Perhaps that's what a son is for.'

Sitting, this hot spring morning, on the escarpment, Bobbie takes out the flint and rolls it in her palm. It fits comfortably, it is comforting, yet she wishes she could penetrate its mystery. Smash a stone in a hundred pieces and each will remain a locked door. She envies those who stumble upon artefacts – the arrowheads and axes of the deep past. They know what they've found. She knows nothing about her stone.

Her father has taught her about the polished flints of the Neolithic. How people would have dug for days through chalk, using red deer antlers as picks, scraping away with the tines, then hacking through top- and wallstone seams, into the floorstone, and finally gouging out nodules of flint. Holding one of these, gauging its strength and character, the craftsman knocked at the flint's door and listened for its answer – would it serve? He would pit stone against stone, knocking away the nodes and bunions, chippings fine as fish scales falling away, until the stone fish of the axe-head swam into his hand.

Nothing of the sort has turned up in Bagshot. But they must be here, under the rust-coloured sand. Tools of the ancient past, waiting to be unearthed.

Rev Rachel, in mufti, has invited him into the garden to partake of breakfast. 'To celebrate this glorious sunshine.' He sits, burying his hands between his thighs. Croissants, freshly squeezed OJ, real coffee.

'This is posh,' he says.

Rachel sinks the plunger and pours him a cup. 'Do you know,' she says, 'it's a month since you moved in. Don't look worried, that's not a prelude to a lecture. I know you'll sort yourself out. You had the gumption to get into the army – to survive out there.'

He watches her closely. 'Yeah,' he says. 'I s'pose so.'

'Tell me about it. The skills you acquired. The talents you discovered you have.'

'Why?'

'To remind you, I suppose, what you're capable of.'

Aitch knows the answer to that question. 'Where should I start?'

'At the beginning. The training, the discipline.'

'It all made sense, didn't it? In Paderborn. I reckoned … it would give me a direction. Like, people would notice me when I got back.'

'Yes.'

'Respect me. But that's bollocks. It's like the way we never got write-ups back home. Because no journalists wanted to tag along for the ride. We'd try sending them films we made on our smartphones. Like this time we called in air support. You could see the gunships lasing their targets. Then boom. Five-hundred pounders. Like the gods were on our side.'

He can sense her discomfort, but why pretend it was otherwise – that they didn't scream for joy when their enemies burned? 'Where's your footage now?' she asks.

'Wiped it when I got home. I'd put it on YouTube but what was the point?'

'Historians might find it interesting.'

'Historians!' Aitch laughs. Oh, that tickles him! 'You think anyone's interested in shaky night footage filmed by some tom in a sangar?'

'It's authentic, filmed by heroes.'

'I'm not a hero.'

'Lots of people would disagree.'

'People are full of shit. It's all "Our Brave Lads", but when you get home you hardly exist. Everyone's got their gadgets and they're laughing at cat gifs and *X Factor* and it's all so fucking trivial, like you want to kick people, you want to shout, because every fucker you see's just so much meat on legs, they're flesh and bone and brain packed in a bag of skin and I know … I've stained your tablecloth.'

'Don't worry about it.'

'I can't even hold a coffee.'

'It'll come out.'

Aitch holds his cup as if it were a small bird that has flown into a window. 'Sorry about the swearing.'

'What swearing? You were very eloquent.'

'Yeah?' There's a new word to describe him. Not so eloquent he can tell her the half of it.

The Rev picks at the shreds of her croissant. 'I want to tell you. I've been in touch with Veterans Aid. There's someone who'd like to meet you.'

It's too soon. She's given him no time. She's pressuring him – just like Bekah, like Stu. He sees the dismay on her face but that's not his fault. Interfering do-gooders. Fucking treehuggers.

'She sounded very friendly. She sees men like you all the time.'

So this is why she laid on the spread. To soften him up before the news. 'I'm going for a run …'

'You have to face it some time. Stay and finish your breakfast.'

'I'm not hungry.' He mumbles an apology and dashes back to his room, to his clobber.

She leaves him to it. No calling his name up the stairs, no tender knock on his door. In five minutes he's ready, shemagh round his neck, the Bergen on his back with a couple of bricks in it to keep him honest. He slips out, taking his spare key, and races down Vicarage Lane, past the last houses, into the pines and the tunnel of trees.

He runs and runs till there's a stitch in his side like someone's opened a zip in his ribs. He slows to a jog. There's acid foam in his mouth. He gobs it into the brambles.

He isn't kind to the Rev. Considering all that she's done for him. Never puts him down. Likes a drink and all. That time he got back from Donnie's to find her on her tod in the living room with a bottle of red and she invited him to join her. Of course her head is full of books. She talks like one of those boffins off the telly. But he likes the way she lets him in, doesn't treat him like some dumb fucker.

'The problem is,' she said that night, 'we've become a society of death worshippers.'

'Of what?'

'James Bond is our saviour. It's all drones and smart-bombs, toys for boys. But the first gods were female. Earth Mother worship is our default spirituality. When you decide that trees and animals are only things for your convenience, you're on the road to destruction. I dare say, when the book gods are forgotten, humans will return to our first beliefs, and who's to say we won't be better off for it?'

'You're a fucking Christian, ain't ya?'

'I *am* a fucking Christian.'

'So isn't that, like, blasphemy?'

'I'm not a fundamentalist, Aitch. I don't do blasphemy. Just doubt. Honest doubt.'

'Our padre didn't have doubts.'

'Good for him. How would they have helped you?'

That was the one time she'd gone heavy on the God stuff. Better than some of the believers he's met. On leave in Dubai, drinking non-alcoholic beer in a shitty bar, that lumbering septic with a goatee guessed he was a soldier, called him over. Bloke said he was a bodyguard in Kabul working for an NGO. Ex-Marine. Tours of duty in Iraq. Aitch was too bored to interrupt him, too sober. The Yank told how he used to lead his squad in prayer. Asking God to ready their souls so they could face danger armed and righteous. The guy leaned in till Aitch could smell his breath. 'Their Allah is a false god. You can't say that in the military but it's true. Their prophet's a false prophet – that's why they have to kill for him. I've seen good men die from IEDs. Blown to shreds below the waist. For what? Longer we're in Afghan, the more these sand niggers gonna come back at us five, ten years from now. Maybe if they'd given us the means. Like in Iraq? We were fighting with our hands tied behind our backs. We got weapons to bomb them back to the Stone Age but that ain't our ROE. You're what, now, twenty, twenty-one? I won't live to see it but you might. Because we're soft, they're gonna win. I tell you, the way they breed, there'll be sharia law in Washington by the time you're an old man ...'

Aitch knew it was bollocks, but he also knew where it was coming from. How do you fight people who love death? Who crave it? Aitch hated them for their reckless-ness, and they hated the *gora feringhee*, red-faced foreign-ers, in their country, on their turf. If the tables were turned, wouldn't he do the same as them?

As for the civilians – poor, stony-faced bastards – they had nothing. There'd been a drought for years. Some of them looked like they belonged in the Middle Ages, medi-evals with drones coming at them from the sky. He saw the carnage they endured, the fucking shambles. Scorched rubble of a mud hut. Lumps and shreds of Talib in a black-ened tree. And a boy of four or five, in a red woollen jumper and tracksuit trousers, lying in the blast zone with the top of his head missing. Dust covered the little body and its wound, so that the face, and the scorched cavity of bone, seemed made of cardboard. Now all children he meets have paper skulls. He knows how easily they can be broken.

Run, Aitch, run. With the burden on his back. Through another stitch and a quick, cleansing puke in the heather. He hits the long straight track he was looking for. Follows it till he reaches the clearing where the ancient fort stood. The sun bearing down on him. Nobody about on the wide scrubby shield of the hill. Only a kid in the distance sitting on the ground, staring into the trees.

9

The Heave

Dayup an sleeps broke by a flock of minas all croakin clickin whistlin an Nathin try to sling one out the trees. Lookin bout he see smoke rise westway an kites turnin.

Nathin kiss the pray patches on his shirt an turn to Old Fort for a piss.

Dowd wake next an Malks eyes on him from the heap of limbs. Aban scratch an turn an Becca moan. Hungers eatin at her guts, buttin her with its pointy head sayin, Me me me. Efia put a hand on Beccas eyes. Keep the day out. Keep out the sun that boil the brain in its cauldron of bone. Burrow out of wakins pain. Stay in sleep a minute longer.

Nathins scream shake everyone. Like a spidie when you poke it the group jerk up, Malk with his stick, Aban his an Efia Rona Becca run an Nathins shoutin, Bones bones! By the bank he stand, cock out, face white, eyes bulgin. Pointin at the earth.

Malks first an others after. Nathin look at us then stare at the ground. His piss a dark clot of sand but hes pointin beside it. At the bones juttin out like dead roots.

They trip me up. I kick em, say Nathin. I kick em an theres more fuck oh fuck.

Easy, say Aban.

Efia kneel an touch the bones. Some crit, she say. Maybe donkey. You say crits? Nathins sweatin heavy. Crit bones only?

For show, say Malk. Dead so long even foxy leave em.

No, say Dowd. Thats a femur.

What?

A mans thigh bone.

Oh its a bloke, shout Nathin, its a bloke!

Mans bone my arse, say Malk. Could be any ole corse.

Look, say Dowd an he start scoopin an scrapin into the bone dirt. Theres more than one skeleton.

Lets go, say Malk.

But Dowds still diggin on his knees now like a dog or coon, the sand flyin an bones barely hid risin like yewka shoots out the bank. Stop it, say Malk, its ole its done.

Look, say Becca an from the place where hill an ground meet a skulls upper come rollin over. Rona Becca Aban Efia crowd bout so Dowds diggin in shadow. *Stop*, say Malk an Nathins holdin his head, tearin at his hair, the sweat on him thick an, Its a sign, he say, its death comin after us. First the kites now this its a *sign*.

Shut yer gob, say Malk. Its just an ole bone dump.

But we sleep on em, say Nathin. We sleep on corses I *piss on em* they gonna rage gainst me gonna come after me –

Enuf now, say Efia, an Dowd look over his shoulder when she touch him an all on a sudden its like his string go, he kneel still an pantin. Bones big as sticks, small as twigs, lyin about. Aban take a second skull an gouge the sand out its eyeholes. There are many people buried, say Dowd, in this old fort.

So leave em, say Malk breakin up Dowds shade. Leave hid whats hid.

What if Nathins right, say Becca, an we curse for diggin em up?

Bad place, say Nathin, bad place.

Not bad, say Malk. One place is lots of places if you wait long enuf. Aint no good place nor bad place. We just flies on em.

Bones dont like disturbin, say Becca. Curse follow us faster an you can walk. Turn bove us like birds.

Peck out our eyes, say Nathin.

Fucks sake *shut it*. Aban turn to Malk say, Get that ouster on his feet. Diggin bout like a poxy dog.

Arrowheads, say Dowd like he hear nuthin Aban just say. Pinchin between finger an thumb two rusty iron points. He wink at em an hold em to the light.

Aban put down the dug up skull. Lets go, he say. Roads waitin an we best be off before suns too hot.

Malk scowl to see the group all gree. Why Abans word carry now not his? Nathins tremblin still an Malk say to him, You scaredy crow. Fuckin girlyman Nathin.

Malk –

Shut yer gob an get the dewcloths.

Campment clear quick away. Packs up an Aban hold the guidin stick while Rona Efia Becca take rations an quipment an Nathin Malk load saltmeat, the tarp, the dewcloths wrung out into jercans. No eatin yet nor none till suns up an hotter. Then rest an maize or piggly pears. Hard grub for the hard trek.

South we go thru juniper scrub an the carders windin up they heat music. Rona follow Aban head down case grub show up. Efia wait for Becca where she trampin slow behind.

Wasser matter, say Efia, why you draggin? Becca shush

her with a finger an scratch at the scabby rash on her arm. Becca, say Efia, why you actin like you gone looper?

Not actin, say Becca her voice low an eyes shifty. Bad luck innit. Fendin gainst the dead. They spirits find you.

Not us, say Efia. We dint mean bad.

Maybe not but look. Butterflies. They followin us.

They aint.

Cos they spirits of the dead. You know its true. Like dragonflies sew up yer lips with twine an roaches nest in yer throat if you sleep with yer gob open.

Well, say Efia, so we go fast an shufty. Leave em bones behind.

Nathins to blame, say Becca. He dig em up.

Nathin hear this an, Im not, he say runnin back thru grass an ashes. Aint my bad nor dont you say so Becca.

Bad lucks on us all then, say Malk comin after. Stand up to it together. Groups stronger than lonesum.

We find the road soon. Or it find us. Davys Way.

Aban go first an Dowd after, tho not as one. Nathin his face hot an wet say to Efia, Its that new bloke. Dowd. He come on us an first nights in a bone dump.

Efia look ahead at the tall stridin boy. Cant find it in her to gree with Nathin tho shes also fraid of curses. Malks pist at you, she say to change the talks walk.

Maybe Im pist at Malk.

Youd never dare, say Becca an Nathin look at her like he want to push her in the road an give her a kickin. Yeah, he say, its all that fuckin ousters fault.

Two miles we cover. Speakin little once the suns up. Sand shimmerin ahead. Efia pull at the bark peelin off a yewkas trunk. How trees sunburn too. Like Efias skin when long ago with Lan she scape from hitchin.

Come the hottest of the day we halt. Drink from our jercans the last of Winnel water an nightspit from the dewcloths. Eat a bite. Moan as bellies wake to say, More but there is none. Malk tell Dowd to feed his self. These our rashuns, he say, dig for yer own ouster boy. Yet Efia slip Dowd some lizard meat.

Grub gone we rest under yewkas next to Davys Way. Rona singin soft, Becca Nathin thinkin on ghosts an Malk on Dowd whos kneelin with his hands in the dust. Efia go to sleep but a scritchy sound wake her. Its Aban. Hes got his red flint in one hand an Feos knife in the other. Lookin hard at his stone. Scorin it with his knifes point. Efia dont ask him what hes doin. She lie back an listen to the carders song. Minutes pass slow. Eyes close. Heads nod.

Malk, say Dowd. Aban look!

Efia groan, Wasser matter? Dowd take her arm an point up the road where a figures sittin. Back to a tree stump. A bloke maybe tho hard to say. Bony for show. A rag bloke in a stainy curta, his skin like a dog or crow just dig him up. Aban shudder an press gainst Malk whisperin, Davy? Is it Davy? But Malks not sayin. He step up, step back, grip his sharpstick an yell, Hoy! The rag bloke dont move. Wassup, say Malk, you in trouble? Still the figure dont move, dont say nuthin, just sit there facin us.

Best go see, say Efia.

What an if, say Nathin, hes a juntaman? Could be a trap. He bring us over an nets drop on us an bastards got him a fresh batch of slaves.

Could be hes got stuff for trade, say Efia. Hut someplace or he know the land an its ways.

Malk say, Right an all gree to see the bloke up close. Malk Aban Nathin go first an Rona take the sling, Dowd a yewka stick he pick up. When we get to the bloke we see hes an old git, all munchy gob an drippy eyes, his skin sunk an arms like they got no flesh in em. The bloke dont seem to mind us standin there, he stare straight up Davys

Way to West Cunny like hes guessin our direction. When Aban speak he dont flinch nor look up tho Abans voice is soft an Efia feel it in her gut like a twist of hunger.

Wasser matter, say Aban, you hurt?

The old bloke say nuthin, dont twitch, so Aban say, Where you from eh? Sted nearby is it? Brag Nell or Bad Shot? Watcher doin out here on a hotten ole feller like you an no water nor nuthin to keep you?

The old bloke dont move, only the skin twitch in his neck like his pulse live up there. Efia reach in her pack for grub but Malks hand stop her. Malk aim his sharpstick so it point close to the old blokes eyes. You lone or what, say Malk. Cos if you got mates dont mean us good –

Malk!

The old bloke reach behind him. Its like a piece of earth just come to life an all step back but Malk who jab his stick. From the tree stump behind him the old bloke pull out a blade. Sharp thing of iron. Good for cutting, like butchers use. Big enuf to gut a man. Whoa, say Malk you hold it there.

The old bloke do like hes told. Holdin the blade out, his arm like its a heavy weight, an then without lookin up or openin his gob he tilt the handle towards us. Like hes makin a gift of it.

What, say Malk. You tradin that?

The old bloke lift his head like to meet Malks eyes. Nearly meet em. Each balls gone milky. Cloudy eyes see nuthin maybe. The blokes other hand stir in the dust, it lift slow like its twice the blades weight an two fingers rise to his throat an scrape the skin there.

Fuck, say Aban.

Again the old bloke drag his fingers cross his throat. Hes looper, say Malk downin his sharpstick.

He want you, say Nathin, to bleed him.

Shut up.

He want you to cut him Malk.

Shut yer gob Nathin!

The old blokes arm with the blade in its still up tho tremblin now with effort. What, say Becca steppin closer, what you wanna die for?

The dusty face thats done nuthin so far split. It crack, like mud in the sun, into a grin. A leer.

Hes old, say Nathin. No more use to no one just a belly to fill. Crawl out on the heave an feed the crows aint that right feller?

With effort the old bloke lift up the arm with the blade in it till its in Malks reach an Malk lash out, knock the tremblin hand, bash the blade out its grip an it fall on the ground between em.

Sicko bastard, say Malk lookin from face to face cross the group. Efia. Rona. Lookit this ole peedo. Aint got balls to end his poxy life.

Leave him, say Becca.

Aint got balls. Stinkin *looper*, say Malk an he spit on the old bloke. Then like this aint enuf he reach down an fling sand in his face.

We stand lookin at the spit an sand on the old blokes face. All but Nathin. He stare at the old blokes eyes, how they gone down like his arms, an its like no words find him like hes asleep. Malks speakin still cos hes shamed of the fear in him an Nathin look at the drop blade, at the old bloke, the group standin bout him like its a dream we sharin, an Nathin find hes bendin down. His knee by the blade, his fingers walk till they stumble on stone. His fingers close over a flint. Nathin look at Malk sayin black words at the old bloke. Malks eyes hid by land shinin behind him. All cross the heave the suns poundin an Nathins blood poundin with it, like its too hot to hold in his body an poundin in his skull, Malks voice an voices of all of us callin him a scaredy crow, a girlyman.

Nathins flint catch the old bloke on the cheek. The man jerk an his cheeks white a sec, then out the blood creep. Nathins standin like hes still throwin the flint, he see the blood come out of the blokes face. Malk stare up Nathins arm an Nathin see the look an down he bend again, the sun throbbin in his skull, an scoop stones up an grit. He throw the lot an the old bloke inch back then sit still, the blood tricklin down his face. Nathin scream at the old bloke, then Malks screamin then Aban. The boys holler an the girls start up an all on a sudden theres more stones flyin. Efia see Rona Becca bend an throw an Malks findin sharp flints, Abans launchin stone after stone, his body twistin like Malairs got him. The old bloke put up his scrawny arms as stones knock him an bite an Efias throwin now an Malk hurl a great rock an the old blokes gob open like a snakes when you stick it an theres a hole in his scalp sprayin red mist.

Stop, say Dowd. *Stop it.*

But its like we dont hear an the old blokes tryin to screw into a ball an the stones bite till they dont seem to hurt him no more an its like tossin stones at a log or an anthill. Dowd lean on Abans arm so Aban start like a dreams just let him go. Malk stop an Becca Rona Efia but Nathins bendin for more an he lift his head to look at what hes done. From the old bloke come a scratchy sigh. He shudder an go stiff, theres a stink from his curta an alls still alls done. Only Nathin pantin, the group in his sights an, Whos a girlyman now, he say. Whos a scaredy crow now?

Its, say Malk. Its what he ask for innit. Its what he want us to do.

Aban turn an start up Davys Way. Efia look after him. Wait, say Becca an shes pickin up the packs.

Lets go, say Rona but Malks gapin at the blood an the sand soakin it up an Rona take him by the hand. Beccas got her rashuns, Efias after her draggin her pack an Abans whos already far into the shimmer down the road.

You may speak of curses now, say Dowd, an he kick dust at Nathins feet.

Dont mean nuthin, say Nathin. Just speed his dyin is all. Some ole sod an now hes gone. Nathin look a last at the corse then sense hes on his lonesum. Wait for me, he shout. Flyin from what we done. The old mans deathday. His birthin back to nuthin.

<hr />

After the Fast Time folk reckon the land starve, the waters shrink an thats why the steds gone small an theres ruins everyway of what once stood. The worlds a corse of what it were, so you got to make friends with the bones cos what else is there. The bones an stones is all. Stones as they always bin an Rona Becca Aban Malk Efia Nathin Dowd walkin on em. Chasin dusk long Davys Way. Hardly speakin to keep gobs wet. Heads clear of all thinks save the guidin stick in Ronas hand an maybe what grub to eat come dark. Then its group or plain sleep like a deep blue river. Only the heave have other plans for us, it up an bite well before the sun bury itself. The whisperin scrub wake an shiver. Then yewkas start bendin an swayin. The group tight up as wind yank the carpet of stones from under our feet. Sand an dust an twigs go flyin. Grit in yer face an hoods boomin. Have to walk crabwise then. Chew grit. Spit sand. Shout so you can hear.

What, say Aban.

Cover, say Rona.

Not under trees, say Becca. They fall an crush us.

Wait, say Efia. Itch.

What, say Becca.

Ditch. Dig down. Trees fall an we get a roof for extras.

All watch Efia as she lean into the wind up the roadside lookin. A ditch run where Davys Way meet the boomin trees. Here, she say an all follow after.

Down in the ditch the wind find us an tug at our hair an clothes. But not so strong nor loud. All look from face to face. Pick the dust off our tongues. Nuthin doin but wait for the storm to blow itself out. Ghosts howlin up Davys Way. Pale waves of sand in the failin light. Ditch the best place to sleep out the night. Hunker down.

The storms still lashin when Aban dig a shithole thirty paces from the group. Unload him an buckle up when he find hes trembling, his knees wont hold him, he has to crawl like a baby an all a sudden he cant. Cant be with the rest of us. He see us like fat grubs shelterin gainst the flyin sand. All huddle as one an he cant come near. Not while hes shakin an, whats this, snottin up an weepin like a kiddie. Oh, he say, oh, to tree roots an a scrabblin beetle. No facin Malk Nathin all blubby like this. Whats he even weepin for if not dumb hunger? No harm stayin where he is. No shame waitin for his shame to pass. Kneelin gainst the ditch bank hearin the wind shout, the trees thrash, he close his eyes to think him into blankness. Only a body shift up next to him.

Aban? Got you some grub. Nuthin much only dry cob an last of the meat.

You eat it, say Aban.

Efia hold out the food to him. Its for you.

Reachin for the grub Aban keep his eyes hid under his hood. Look long the ditch to Malk Rona Becca Nathin. Dowd on his lonesum. Aban chew the dry an rotty cob.

Efia take jercan from her backpack. Offer it to him an he drink.

What we done, Efia say. Back then. What we done to the ole bloke. Ask Rona Becca Malk. They dont know what Im talkin bout its like they forgot already.

You do likeways, say Aban. Ole blokes got one road. We help him long it.

But his face, say Efia. The way he drop –

Its done now an over. Hes back where he start from like we gonna be. Dead an all his pain forgot.

Its killin, say Efia.

World take back whats owed it an we just part of the world.

So why you shove off then?

Eh?

Why you run first? An sittin now on yer lonesum? If alls for the good.

Efia look at him hard. Cant read his face in the storm dusk. No thinks comin off it. Cos, he say. Just need to.

Just need to, say Efia like a valley speakin back. What for tho? Hot work bein lonesum. Cooler when all gree.

Its hot sometime, say Aban then stop his mouth.

Hot, say Efia, when?

When all gree.

She nod at this. Tho the words cut deep an she want to send em far away. Rightyer, say Efia but so soft he ask her to say it again. Then Aban find her hand like a bird on his knee. He feel it there an see it. How it move upways. Rightyer, say Efia.

Like a hornid stung him he jolt from her touch. No! Aban –

Groups safest. Best place. Dont go closin us off.

He find no more to say, only the heart in him freakin like a bird in a trap. Shufty back to the group. To Malk

Rona Becca Nathin. That Dowd. Back to the safest place. Wait out the storm there. While it toss its playthins. The heave shakin itself in anger. All push together gainst the bitin. Aban far as can be from Efia tho his thinks are where she is. Till sleep creep over us an trouble for a time leave us be.

10

Blueface

M arcus watched the native priest. He heard him speak and saw the young men listen. Nobody marshalled his gaze or forced it to the ground where, surely, they meant to bury him, Marcus Cornelius Severus, second son of Tertius and Sabina Marciana, decurion of the XIV Twin Legion.

The day was fading already. Above all he feared the loneliness of what awaited him. The absence, between this instant and his last, of a single face to look on him with love.

Already his humiliation was under way. With his hands tied behind his back, he had had no choice but to urinate on himself. The warmth had brought a gross, temporary relief, till all that remained was his stink and the chill of wet wool. He was hungry too, and a thirst indistinguishable from despair furred his mouth. He listened to the hot purpose of the druid. To keep from thrashing in his bonds – to avoid further disgracing himself – he turned his head and tried to catch Glyco's attention.

The cavalryman was asleep. Could it be? Had they –? No, his chest was moving, the bloodied head rose and fell with each breath. Marcus stared. It was unfathomable: to nap when their lives were rationed, to lend to oblivion what soon would belong to it for ever. He wanted, madly, to shout across the clearing, to cut through the diatribe and order his man awake.

Then a thought stung him. Glyco had a plan; he was gathering strength before acting on it. Or else he knew that rescue was on its way. Surely traffic on the road, a tradesman or a messenger, would have seen the blood by now – unless they had covered it up with snow – but then it would have seeped through. Only soon it would be dark. Even if the alarm were raised, what chance of rescue so late in the day? No, Marcus barked at the hope in his chest. Do not kindle. Do not burn.

He tried to persuade himself that he was dead, that the little time he had left was posthumous, a respite from the nothingness which was already his. A ghost clothed in flesh, he took gulps of air to savour its sweetness. He looked at the fallen needles of yew, and how the ice that furred them was made of the frailest crystals. It was his task to pay attention – for all this was about to be taken away for ever.

A fit of terror shook him, made his teeth chatter till they drummed in his skull, and he raged against himself for this lack of self-mastery. He sent his thoughts home: to his father and brother at the warehouse, to Elpis, his old nurse, asleep beneath the olive trees. He watched his parents, with all the household behind them, receive the news of his disappearance. He saw the wheatfield behind the villa, the dark candles of the cypress trees in the burial ground of his ancestors. His grandparents, cousins, the stillborn twins, were bound in earth that would never hold him. Instead – what? This sand for a grave? The slime of a British bog?

The druid's speech climbed a crest and the conspirators cried out, three times, a word in their language that Marcus knew:

'*No*.'

He fixed his working eye on Glyco and this time it was admiration he felt, almost love, for the man's defiance. To turn the weakness of sleep into a weapon, to show the rabble his contempt for its frenzies.

He sensed that he was being watched.

It was the boy.

Marcus had given him little thought. Why did they hold him captive? Was he the son of a rival tribe? Was he a spy to merit his bruised cheek?

The boy held his gaze for an instant, then looked away.

Together and apart, boy and soldier watched the druid. Whatever else he had lost, the man retained his cauldron of hot words. He reached into it and his audience was spellbound, its nerves and sinews stiff with listening. Marcus was able, with what Condatis had taught him, to pick out some of the words: 'foreigner', 'father', 'shame'. It was the straightest path for a firebrand, to probe the live wound between generations.

Marcus listened, and curiosity made a clearing in the forest of his dread. He noticed how like his wolfhound the druid looked: his hair thick and tangled, the black turning to grey, his starved frame lean and loping. He remembered from stories how the crazed warrior, by resembling the bull, the horse, the wild boar, took on the animal's strength. He found himself marvelling at his enemy, wondering about the road which had brought him here, to pacified country and this senseless act of rebellion. The druid had been an imposing figure once. Somewhere, to judge by the damage to his leg, he had come to physical harm. Still, with his cavernous voice and burning eyes, with the priestly torc under his winter rags, he made one forget that he was a vagabond, a speck of ash from a conflagration. A ghost, like Marcus, outstaying his welcome in the world.

He saw the druid hand something to one of the boys. What was that? It looked like a pouch.

Suddenly he wanted not to see. He wanted to be asleep like Glyco. The druid removed his gaze, very briefly, from his audience and sent it, swift as a hawk and with the same intent, towards his captive. Marcus saw, and then doubted he had seen, a smile on the man's face. Then, from the seemingly fathomless recesses of his cloak, the druid extracted a noose of rope and gave it to the brute. To the redhead he handed a long dagger.

Marcus strained against his bonds. He fought stupidly, in panic and indignation, trying with what strength he retained to break the cords that held him down.

It was no use. As quickly as it had entered his body, the fight went out of him. He let the stake hold him up. He hung aslant the frozen earth, and a phrase he had heard many times from old soldiers in Aquitaine came into his head: 'If your end is come, drink bravely of death.'

It had sounded easy then. What if he begged for mercy – disgraced himself in front of Glyco? His ghost would never rest from such dishonour.

The strange boy was watching him.

'Keep your eyes to yourself, brat!'

The boy looked away, not for shame but because the druid's speech was done.

Oh gods. The young men were looking his way. As one they turned; they bent their bodies in haste. But they did not come at him with their weapons. It was their injured colleague who called them. They gathered about him, the druid following.

It was difficult, through the press of bodies and in the dying light, to see what was happening. The injured lad cried out; he was in agony and it was agony to hear him. His comrades flapped about helplessly, they added what clothes they could spare, in this cold, to his cocoon of furs and leather. Why did the druid not do more to help? They were hidden in woods: the green wall of yews would conceal any fire … unless. Unless it suited the priest for his disciple to suffer. Marcus wished he had not drawn his sword: he had done his enemy a service in using it. The druid made a show of attending to the boy's wound. The clouts strapped about the head were gross with blood. The stricken face dragged and stared, eyes rolling into its skull. The druid prayed in silence, then gave orders, sending the boys hither and thither in search of medicinal plants and water. It was a laudable performance: the killer as healer, ministering to the servants of his revenge.

The heavy youth, set on his mission, walked close to Marcus and let his fist drag against the decurion's injured eye.

The pain was revelatory – the dragging of iron spurs through livid flesh. Marcus sobbed. He bit his cheeks to silence himself until he tasted blood.

He rocked himself as well as he could to see off the pain. He was aware of bodies moving about the grove, the rush and patter of orders in action. When he dared open his good eye, he saw the tall youth, the one with the pouch, watching him. No: he was watching the boy. Even through the clangour of his pain and thirst and fear, Marcus sensed how the presence of the child discomfited the conspirators. This tall one especially.

He looked again at the young captive. He had spoken harshly to the boy and regretted it, for here, alone of all the faces in the grove, was one in which fear appeared to win out over hatred.

The cold pressed like a hand on the earth. The sky was clear, with stars like thrown salt. Andagin squirmed to break the mould of his aching body; his teeth clattered in his head; his fingers and toes were blunted stumps. He wondered if he might die and thought, not of his parents or relatives, but of the cow in her byre with her wet snout and grassy breath. He tried to imagine himself against her warm flank.

Aesu groaned in his shroud of furs. Lugh sat beside him. Barocunas was helping the man of art, handing him ribwort plantain for a poultice.

A tawny owl hooted as his brother returned from the wood. Judoc knelt before the man of art and whispered. Andagin guessed, and blushed to guess, what he was asking for. He saw his brother come towards him with a skin of water.

Andagin swallowed the bitter coldness that hurt his teeth. 'Give it to the soldiers,' he gasped.

'No.'

'They must have water.'

'They can eat snow.'

'You know it is never enough.'

'Forget about the soldiers. You give me trouble enough. I am to keep you under watch.'

'What can I do? I am trussed up like them.'

'For your own good,' said Judoc. 'I suppose you heard what our master said?'

'I understood nothing. Please, *please* let me go home. I will say I hurt my leg and this kept me away. It will pain them all to be worrying for me.'

'I cannot.'

'But I promise –'

'This is *my* path you walk in. That is my cloak. I am your elder and you will obey.'

Andagin's chest filled with bad air. He fought to keep his eyes from flooding.

'I have something for you,' said Judoc.

He saw his brother reach into the recesses of his hide. 'I do not want it!'

'Still, I think you might.'

Judoc held out a clenched fist. He turned it over and opened his fingers. The stone lay in the cradle of his palm.

Andagin stared.

'Take it.'

'Where did you find her?'

'Where it fell. Here.'

Andagin felt the intimate weight in his palm. He travelled its contours, the carvings his thumb knew. The tears came fast now: he made no effort to stop them.

'I thought. It was gone. For ever.'

'Some things come back. What do you think it is?'

'I cannot say.'

'Because you do not know?'

'Because some things must not be spoken.'

'Well. Much good may it do you.'

Judoc stood up. It was not possible in the half-light to see the expression on his face. 'Will you be warm enough in your two cloaks?'

'I think so. Will Aesu –?'

'That is for the gods to decide. You understand … Andagin, I must join the others.'

'Yes.'

'If you need me in the night – if you lose the feeling in any part of yourself –'

'I will whisper.'

'And I will hear you.'

Andagin watched his brother sink into darkness. He felt calm and clear-headed, as in the past, when a fever had burned itself out in his blood. The stone did this; the Goddess was with him, and in her stillness Andagin pushed through a tangle of thorns.

He knew what had been done and what was to follow. These bloodied foreigners – the sleeping one and the other who looked at him now and then – were as good as dead. The dark waters would take them. But they were not to be the only sacrifices. His parents, his cousins and friends, would pay with their lives for the lives taken. This was the lesson taught in the east, that the madman ignored in his rage. Perhaps it was too late already. Yet if Andagin saved these two – if a whelp of a tribesman brought these soldiers home – there might yet be mercy for the innocent. Reprisals could lose them everything: their homes, their land. But not their lives. Not the lives of those he loved.

It fell to him, to him alone. Everything he knew trembled like a spider's thread at the pressure of a blade. His world. His mother. Nyfain. His da. Let them not burn the heath and salt the meadows; let them spare the fort of his ancestors.

He would have to betray his brother.

'Why are you weeping?' Barocunas stood above him. 'The master will not keep you. When the deed is done you will be free. I am sure of it.'

'Perhaps,' said Andagin, whose guts would hold no food, 'you could find some meat for me.'

He had to do it. He had no idea how. He was alone in the cold world.

'Judoc! Judoc!'

Voices hissed and barked for silence. Still Andagin cried out, as if he had done himself an injury.

'Brother!'

'You will give us all away.'

'I cannot feel my hands. The binding is too tight. Let me be free of it.'

Judoc breathed hotly into his face. 'Will you be quiet at last if I do?'

'Yes.'

'And you will obey me in everything?'

'I will.'

His brother knelt beside him. Close enough to touch. 'Do I have your word you will stay in this place until we have finished our work?'

'You have it. I am so cold my fingers burn.'

Judoc left him and Andagin feared he would not come back, or might do so with the seer to consult on the request.

His brother returned with a blade and cut through the cordage. Andagin was glad of the cold and the pain in his body, for they made sense of his sobbing.

'There. You are free now, stop crying.'

'Thank you.'

'And here is your pack.' Judoc dropped it into his lap. 'There is no food. Do you know we fast tonight?'

'I know nothing.'

'So you must go hungry like the rest of us. You are *with* us now. Do you understand? Our crime is yours. I never meant this for you but you followed me. We are both wanted men.'

'Yes.'

'Our lives do not belong to us.'

As soon as Judoc had gone, Andagin opened his pack and felt inside. The knife had been taken. Still, his hands were free. He buried them beneath his two coats. Under cover he warmed the stone with his cold, sluggish fingers.

Bring strength to me. Bring me courage, Mother.

From the shivering, hungry, night-drowned camp, a voice rose in wheedling protest. It sounded like Lugh: 'We must light a fire. We *must*.'

'No fires.' That was the madman. Andagin could just make him out, huddled in furs with his great hound. 'We must purge ourselves by this waiting.'

'The cold will be fatal to him.'

'Hush now.'

'It will *kill* him.' Bodies wrestled and whispered. Lugh was not to be silenced: 'Why do we not do it now? Make the sacrifice so Aesu may be saved.'

The deep voice of the seer was not so gentle. 'It has to be done in a fitting way to please the powers. Be quiet, Kei. Your cousin raves but there is no pain, for I have seen to that. Kei, will you be *still*?' For the wolfhound had joined its whimpering to the men's voices; it whined and loosed a deep bark, which its master answered with a kick.

The hound was not put off. It bayed at the stars. Barocunas came running.

'The soldier is gone!'

There was silence for a time, save for the hound's almost joyful noise. Andagin looked across the trampled, frozen grass. It was the other, the bald and bloodied one. The nearer captive sat hunched, letting his bonds and the stake hold him up.

'To it, boys,' cried the seer. Aesu and his suffering were forgotten. 'Barocunas, Lugh – take Kei. He will find the scent. Judoc, see that he is caught, and quickly. Kill him if you must, we still have the other.'

The hound was in the woods already. Bodies rushed out of the grove after it, while Aesu gibbered alone in his dying.

Andagin left his place against the tree trunk. He crawled in darkness to the stake where the remaining soldier was captive. With his teeth he pulled the mittens off his hands; he felt with naked fingers for the knots in the rope. If the madman came their way now – if he checked on the bindings of his lone captive – all was lost.

Andagin's fingers were deft despite the cold. A knot eased, though it hurt as if he were tearing his fingers on stone. The seer was with Aesu, tending to him. Andagin breathed into the soldier's hands as he picked and tugged. The man must formerly have been unconscious, for he stiffened with awareness of the boy. Andagin put a hand on the man's shoulder and pressed a trembling finger to his foreign lips.

He worked the knots loose. Now he urged the captive to his feet. The soldier stumbled and winced. Cold and his position had made an old man of him.

Andagin held tightly to the soldier's hand. They sought a gap in the wall of yew.

The branches clutched and dragged. He feared the soldier would not get through. The yews resisted, whispering – then let go.

Boy and soldier said nothing. The man seemed to recognise his chance. They stumbled blindly into the wood.

11

No Man's Land

Now *that* shouldn't be here. Did someone plant the bulb last winter? Or could a jay have stolen it from a garden and stowed it forgetfully on the heath?

Bobbie kneels before the late daffodil and touches the moist silk of its petals. An outsider, exotic almost beside the ling and gorse. Contemplating the flower, she imagines the plenitude of summer on its way. Nightjars will return to their breeding grounds, trailing their hot purr from Africa. She hears goldfinches squabble, a murmur of bees, the cluck of a cock-pheasant in the scrub below the ramparts. Finally, a cuckoo! The robber bird, so rare these days, has made it through Sahel drought and sandstorms, past hunting rifles and lime traps, over warm seas and cold, to this hillside.

She shuts her eyes and lifts her face to the sun. The world glows blood orange; nothing but a film of skin between her and the home star. The same light is opening the chestnut leaves. She can hear the sap rising. It drums inside the clotted buds, a pulse forcing them open, capillaries filling with juice.

Would she notice this if her grandfather had not alerted her to it? Long ago, holding her small hand in his, pointing up at the branches. He is beside her now. She senses it in her shoulders …

A man is watching her. Young, clean-shaven. A tangle of tattoos on his arms. He wears a beige T-shirt, combat trousers and what look like army boots. Also – strangely, given the weather – a grey patterned scarf.

*

He tries a smile and thinks better of it. He doesn't want to frighten her.

The girl gets up. Spiky short hair like a boy. Bites and bruises on her legs. 'I thought I was the only one here,' she says.

'Me too.' He keeps his hands where she can see them. No sudden moves. 'Funny to think we're a few miles from Bracknell town centre.'

She looks up at him and there's no judgement in her eyes. Kind eyes. Chestnut brown. He sees her notice the twisters in his trousers, his polished boots. 'Are you a soldier? I'm just wondering. There are lots round here, with Sandhurst and the ranges.'

'I used to be,' Aitch says. 'Princess of Wales's Royal Regiment, First Battalion. You, uh, military?'

'I'm only twelve.'

'I mean your family.'

'Hardly. My mother works for the government. International development.'

'Oh yeah, treehuggers.' Dipstick! 'What's your dad do?'

'He's an archaeologist.'

'Like Indiana Jones?'

'Not so much fighting. Like, when they want to build a road, they sometimes dig up old bones or ruins. That's when my dad comes in. He evaluates the find –'

'You got the big words, ain't ya?'

'– and records what's down there, so when they build over it, people know about it.'

'What's the point? If everything gets buried again?'

The girl shrugs. 'It's progress,' she says.

                              *

Bobbie should be wary of strangers. Why would a guy like this want to talk to her? He's just being polite. Few people in the woods, the fort unvisited: it would be rude not to pass the time of day. Her instincts are quiet. Soldiers exist to protect us, don't they?

'This site,' she says, 'is of archaeological significance.'

'Yeah, I know.'

'Of course Caesar's Camp is a misnomer.'

'Miss Who?'

'As Julius Caesar never actually conquered Britain, he just visited it.'

'Bloody tourists. Mind you, all the emperors were called Caesar.'

'Well,' she says, taken aback. 'But this was never a Roman settlement. It was built as a defensive fort by ancient Britons.'

'You gonna be a school teacher when you grow up?'

'It's my dad. He knows these things.'

'Not about, is he?'

'He does know I'm here.'

She sees a flicker of worry on the soldier's face, as if he can tell that he has just scared her a little. 'I'm Aitch,' he says.

'Aitch?'

'Short for Harry.'

'I'm Bobbie, short for Roberta.'

'All right, Bobbie.'

'All right.'

*

He watches her bend at the waist and give a shin a good scratch. Looks satisfying.

'So you know all about this place,' he says, winning her trust, making her proud of herself. He tries this on Barry, or used to when he still saw the lad. 'I bet you're as smart as a whip, ain't ya?'

'Are you from nearby?'

'Just down the road. Used to bike round here when I was a youngster. Motocross, you know.'

'My dad hates motorbikes.'

'No one's perfect.'

She asks him how well he knows the heath. What heath? All of it – the place they're standing in. 'Dunno. I've always known it, not paid it much attention.'

She grins at him with what looks like mischief. 'Do you want to see something?'

'Sure.'

She beckons him to a gorse bush. He tells her what it is, in case she thinks he's a total div.

'There's this game,' she says. 'Well, it's not a game, just a fun thing. Look.' Aitch watches as she stretches a finger towards the yellow flowers. She picks one out. 'You have to press on the lower petal. Imagine you're a bee.' The gorse flower pops under the pressure of her finger and a tiny yellow mist escapes. She repeats the action with two new flowers and both open with a spray of pollen. 'You have a go,' she says.

Aitch does. A silent snap – a puff of yellow on his fingernail. He chuckles and now they're both doing it, going at
the flowers like kids popping bubble-wrap.

'If my mates could see me now. Tickling flowers like
some Rupert.'

She looks at him. 'What's a Rupert?'

'Commissioned officer. It's what we call 'em. Not to
their faces, that'd be insubordination.'

'Why Rupert? Like the bear?'

'Dunno, it's a posh name. Like Roberta.'

That was worth the risk: she laughs, not at all offended.
He has a go at one more flower before he notices that each
one, after it's been depressed, hangs open like a jaw gaping
on its broken hinges. That flipflop they caught trying to
launch an RPG. Aitch smashed his jaw with his rifle butt.
How it swung from his head as they dragged him into the
belly of the Snatch.

'Here,' he says, 'can I ask you something?'

'Depends.'

He tells her that, when he saw her, he thought she was
talking to herself. She blushes.

'I suppose I was talking to my grandfather.'

'Where's he, then?'

'He's dead. I wasn't really talking to him, just imagining
I was.'

'I used to do that. When you're fighting there's a voice,
but it's yours. I dunno how to explain it. You talk back.'

'To yourself?'

'With yourself. It doesn't mean you're crazy, it means
you're trying to get through it.'

Come off it, Aitch. Why would she want to hear any of
this? She's just humouring him, being polite. Maybe she's
scared of him, and with reason. There's no one about – he
could drag her into the scrub and rape her.

Just thinking this, it's as if a lid of lead comes down over his head. He looks at her, this child, a virgin, and realises there's no one to stop him.

'Look,' he says, 'you've got somewhere to get to, ain't ya?'

'Not really.'

'Sure you have. You got family waiting for you.'

'Only my dad.'

'I bet he's wondering where you are.' She doesn't even have tits. Not the first buds of them. 'Listen,' he says. 'Listen, thanks for the nature lesson.'

She looks bewildered.

Now he's running. Legging it. Closet nonce. Scarpering from a tomboy.

Only when the girl is lost behind trees does he slow to a walk. About time, too – he's gasping for breath. Not a click of ground covered and he's sweating like a pig.

He's unfit. The only place he's running to is fat. Fat fucking disgrace.

What freaked him out? What spooked him?

The darkness inside. Preening its black feathers. How does he know the instinct survives in him to keep him from crossing the line? He's done it before.

It began with just another fuck-up. An everyday ambush – VCP, government soldiers, but his team got sent in to mop up. They didn't even have decent armour. Only the Snatches were fit for purpose, and that purpose wasn't saving the lives of British toms. Aitch travelled in the rear Snatch, Chris and Gobby rode up front with a mobile armour everyone called Scoot. He was ten metres behind them. Saw their Snatch leap up – a black cloud tipping it on its side.

He was out and running before he could think. Bits and pieces were still falling when he and Dan got to them.

Scoot was torn to shreds, a smoking torso in the front of the wreckage. Chris was screaming as Dan burrowed into the Snatch to get to him. Aitch looked to Gobby, his mate since the first day in Paderborn. He'd been thrown clear of the vehicle and was out cold. His leg had been torn off above the knee. Aitch actually looked for it, as you might for a missing boot. Rolfie had abandoned the wheel and was shouting into the side of Aitch's head as they dragged Gobby to the second Snatch. He strapped field dressings to his stump. Gobby smelt of shit and fireworks. They got the IV in, morphine, jacket over him for warmth, a roll mat under his neck.

Dan came back from the fragged Snatch with Chris over his shoulder and unloaded him on the floor of the Land Rover. Chris was covered in smoking wounds – too many to know where to concentrate the dressings. He was shaking and gasping and his eyes rolled. Dan had to slap Aitch about the helmet before he could reconnect with his training. His hands were tacky with blood.

Rolfie was back at the wheel and he gave no warning before turning the Snatch around. Aitch tipped over with the momentum and lay on the floor, in the blood bilge, while Dan checked Gobby for a pulse and tried to reassure Chris. 'You can hack it, mate. You're going home. Selly Oak and a hero's welcome.' Chris was losing colour. His hands shook near his face like the mandibles on a crab. 'Don't worry about a thing, mate. Gobby here's taking a nap, the lazy cunt. We'll get you back in no time, they'll patch you up ...'

Aitch remembers tearing towards the drop zone, the dust cloud churned up by the Slick's rotors. Getting the lads on board.

That night in Camp Bastion, the CO came to see them. They were meant to be watching a DVD but Aitch couldn't make sense of the film. Gobby and Chris were dead. They'd succumbed to their wounds before their Hercules reached Karachi.

The next day they went out on patrol. They'd insisted – they were professionals. It's what their mates would have expected. The village was friendly, which pissed them off because they were itching for a fight, or at least to make arrests, knock some fucking heads together.

It wasn't much of a village. More like a giant had shat houses and kicked his turds over a hillside. There was one place they didn't like the look of, east of the others, in a leafless orchard. A sixth sense had them braced for trouble before it came.

Everyone made it to cover behind a mud wall while the bullets zipped past, snapping and cracking in the air. That's when the drill kicked in. They lay down suppressing fire with the Minimis while Rolfie called for back-up. Then the Minimis stopped. Aitch saw it for himself through a crack in the wall. He'd heard of the practice but never seen it, not in a contact.

Between them and the militants, two elderly women cowered, their heads bowed, their arms half raised in surrender or prayer. Human shields. Probably they'd been pushed out of the orchard the moment the firing started. They stood in the open like beasts awaiting slaughter.

The flipflops stopped firing so they could be heard. 'Eh British! We blow up your friends!'

'Fuck,' said Rolfie.

The old women had worked out where Aitch and the lads were sheltering. They looked towards them, their hands open. Aitch could see their grey palms.

'We kill your friends, British!'

Rolfie opened fire. It was contagious. Aitch let rip with his SA-80, Brewster and Dan with the Minimis. All four of them shooting into the trees, blasting away till dead man's click.

The dust. The quiet. The orchard was tattered. They reloaded and walked over.

The elderly women were dead. From the way they lay, it was obvious who had done it.

They entered the orchard in a kind of daze. Two dead flipflops. AK-47s. Trees oozing sap where their bullets had cut into them.

'We had no choice,' Rolfie was saying. 'It was them or us.'

They'd had no choice, but even so they needed a common story. Rolfie was talking sense into them. Explaining what had just happened. Brewster said nothing, Dan said nothing. Aitch nodded, his mouth so parched that he couldn't speak. He nodded, while the dust turned black beneath the bodies of the women.

———

Five minutes from Caesar's Camp, picking up the ghost of a signal, her mobile bleeps. She has to back into the shade to read the screen.

WHERE ARE YOU?

She quashes the temptation of a petulant reply.

Im at C camp
heading home.
Xx

Given how slowly her father texts – brow furrowed, thumb hesitating over the display – the reply is swift:

MEET ME AT STAR POINT.
ON MY WAY.

Bobbie rereads the text. Maybe he just fancies a walk. She shrugs the rucksack more comfortably on her shoulders and sets off to the rendezvous.

Her father is waiting for her where all the tracks of the forest, like spokes in a wheel, converge. He is in full adventurer mode, binoculars knocking against his chest as he rushes to meet her.

'What do you think you're doing,' he shouts, 'disappearing like that? Bobbie! I had no idea where you were.'

'I took my phone.'

'Out here there's hardly any signal, you know that. You should at least have left a note. Do you hear me? You're a *child*, I'm responsible for you. How am I supposed to protect you if you just wander off like that?'

'You'd gone out!'

'That's beside the point. Look, don't ... Roberta, I'm not scolding you. I just freaked out, OK?'

If he tries to hug her, she'll hit him.

'Listen,' he says. 'I got a call from Mike, the forest ranger. There've been two attempted heath fires near Crowthorne and reports of youths on motorbikes.'

'I've not seen a thing.'

'Well, that's good. Now let me walk you home.'

'You didn't come out here to find me.'

'What?'

'You came out to spy on the heath.'

'What are you talking about?'

'Be a have-a-go hero.'

'I came out because I guessed where you'd be.'

'So if you guessed, why did you freak out when I wasn't at home?'

'Don't interrogate me, Roberta.'

'Let's just go, shall we? Since I need protection.'

His jaw tightens. 'Oh, you have your mother's talent for turning the tables.'

'What does *that* mean?'

'I'm not prepared to argue with you.'

'I don't think you could.'

'You have a serious attitude problem, young lady.'

'Whose fault would that be?'

Her father turns and walks down one of the firebreaks. Bobbie, in sorrow and rage, watches him go, till the growing distance between them tugs her after him.

As they walk, he watches the trees on either side of the track. His pace is too quick for her – she's tired, for heaven's sake.

They have gone half a mile when they hear the engines. Bikers coming on fast. Her father looks back towards Star Point and there they are, three of them, hurtling down the firebreak. Of all the paths available, they chose this one.

Bobbie tugs her father's sleeve.

'Dad.'

'Wait.'

'Dad!'

The front rider wears black leathers with a blue helmet. When her father holds out his arm, the biker stops and puts a boot to the ground.

'What's this?'

'You are biking illegally on protected land.'

The second and third bikers stop. They lift their visors. Teenagers.

'Says who?'

'Under the Highways Act of 1980 –'

'Piss off.'

'– it is an offence to ride motorbikes on common land. Moreover, this is a Site of Special Scientific Interest.'

The bikers look at her father. One stares at Bobbie till she cannot bear to look back.

The front biker revs his engine and the air turns grey and foul.

'You're breaking the law!'

'Why don't you fuck off out of it? It's not your land, is it?'

'I'm telling you what the law says.'

'Are you a police officer?'

'No, but I can summon one.'

'Go on then. Go on, wanker.'

The teenagers rev. They circle Bobbie and her father. He stands his ground, tapping the screen of his mobile. The biker with the blue helmet comes very close. Bobbie feels the wind of him as he passes.

Her father lurches like a striker reaching for a header. He drops to one knee, holding the back of his head.

'Daddy!'

The bikers roar up the firebreak towards the Devil's Highway.

'Daddy!'

He puts a hand to the ground to steady himself. 'Stop clawing at me, for Christ's sake.'

Bobbie steps away. Her right knee is trembling. She sinks her mind into it to make it stop.

'Give me my phone.' Her father rests his hands on his thighs. 'I'll be all right in a moment.'

Bobbie picks up his phone and sleeve-wipes the dusty screen. 'No bars.'

'There wouldn't be. I was trying to intimidate them.'

He gets up slowly. Bobbie hands him the phone and he meets her gaze as he takes it.

NO MAN'S LAND   133

'Don't worry about me.'

'OK,' says Bobbie, but her eyes are stinging, she's letting him down but she can't help it.

'... the back of my skull is harder than that boy's fist.' He puts a reassuring hand on her shoulder. She feels his grip tighten.

The bikers are coming back. Their engines fart in the distance.

He grabs Bobbie's arm and pulls her into the pines. 'Down,' he says and bundles her into a shallow trench. He presses on her head as the bikers roar past. They whoop and holler. Her father peers out but Bobbie cannot lift her head because he is pressing on it with his elbow.

The noise subsides.

'Are they after us? Why'd they come back?'

'We're going to have to stay put for a while.'

She begins to snivel and wipes her face with her sleeve.

Twice more the bikers ride past, as if on patrol. Bobbie and her father improve on their hiding place with a mass of rhododendron. They hide for half an hour, till Bobbie has to pee, squatting in the green stems, her spray fizzing into the soil.

When her father thinks it's safe, they cut through the pines and make for home. They move fast and, by Surrey Hill, Bobbie is out of breath. Even when she complains of a stitch, he says nothing, and this frightens her more than anything.

Safely home, they drink tap water at the sink.

'You need a shower,' Dad says. 'I have phone calls to make – I'm going to be in the study all evening. You can look after yourself, can't you? Watch some television.'

'OK.'

'And don't worry. About what happened. It won't happen again, I promise.'

'I won't tell Mum.'

Her father bites his lower lip. He seems to haul his words up from a great depth. 'I'd appreciate that.'

Hours later, when she is in bed, Bobbie senses or dreams that he is looking in on her, watching silently from behind the bedroom door.

12

The Heave

What now?
Im thinkin.
What now Malk? Becca turn on Aban who hold the guidin stick. You say this track take us all the way to West Cunny. You *tell* us.

Becca, say Rona, cool it.

Malk and Aban have done their best, say Dowd. They led us this far.

An wheres that then? Wheres this stinky place?

All look bout an no thinks clear on the question. Davys Way just peter out. Stop in midst of driftin sand like the lost end of a dream. Elseways every turn nuthin but heave. Loomin over us, a mile of redwoods big like only the Fast Time make em. Aban look at the scorchy trunks, the high branches like dry bones. Still signs of life, more dark rags than boughs an crowns all weird an lightnin struck. He stroll to the nearest an sink his nails in the bark. The trunks wider than a hut, wider than a hunnerd yewkas all bound together. Aban go closer. Find hes pressin his face gainst the bark. His arms wide bout the trunk. Behind him Beccas rantin like she gone looper, Aban rest his cheek gainst the redwood, breathe in its smell, this livin link with all thats gone. Like touchin it might send tree thinks deep into his brain.

Aban. *Oi!*

He turn blinkin. Malks pointin, his face all rage, at the guidin stick. Abans put it down. He put it down like it dont need holdin always. Fuck, he say an grab it up. Grab it up an feel for the guidin in it. Like it could be gone. Seep out cos he let it drop.

Nathins stridin up to him. Aban tremble an hold out the guidin stick, lookin at Nathin Malk Efia. Leastways his forgettin shush Becca. She gape at him like he just piss him an all look to Malk for his say an he say to Nathin, Take it off him.

I forget, say Aban. The shame in him like a knife. The walls of his heart cut by Malks anger. His bro. His bestest from way back. Hiccups shake Aban like hes gonna weep but he nod cos all gree an Nathin get the guidin stick.

Wheres it brung us, say Rona.

Nathin stare at the guidin stick like hes waitin for an answer. It come from Efia.

Look she say. Over there.

All follow her pointin past the redwoods. South an west in amid yewkas a darker stain of green. A stand of palms an willows. A waterin place? Wells an fresh water?

Yeah but, say Becca. Could be trollers an juntamen.

Could be, say Efia. Best chance it tho. Least its some-place what an this way all block up.

So the group change course for the southways waterin. Aban trailin behind huggin his shame. Nathin turnin the guidin stick where Malk tell him to.

At first sound of folk we scamp into hidin. Only these folk carry no sharpsticks nor akays. Kiddies with sacks an barrows. Women carryin babies on they hips. Blokes pushin carts or draggin goats.

Hoofers, whisper Nathin.

Na, say Malk. No lifestock or weapons.

Who then?

Lets ask, say Efia but Rona Becca pull her back. Keep down, say Malk, an with branches screenin us we follow the strangers to see where they headin. Turn out its the green of willows an rushes. Smoke coilin up from cookin fires. Stink of bog grip our noses an we see folk bendin then straightin up with pots sloshin. Water comin from a brown rotty swamp. A foul place draggin trees an crits into it.

Watch yer step, say Malk. Dont wanna sink in there.

The women once they pots full lead us out on a stretch of sand that go to the ruins of a red brick manshun. Whole complex of manshuns. More redwoods in rows marchin up from the swamp. The trunks blast by fire an black as charcoal but high up still some branches leafin. Down at the roots folk everyway. Cookin fires an rough shelters made of sticks an cover with palm fronds an sackin. The lot like some angry wind just blow it here. Dozens to each hut. Old blokes, women, little kiddies. Huddlin under the redwoods. Eatin up every scrap of shade.

Efia wait!

Shes in the open, walkin to the huts. Whats to be fraid of, say Efia. Come on.

Aban only then Dowd follow. Malk Nathin Becca Rona watch. Keepin low to see what happen.

Up the redwood track Efia Aban Dowd keep they heads down. Talismans everyway on sticks in the ground. Heads of birds, grass dolls, strips of lizard skin. See-see boxes from the Fast Time rusty on crumblin walls. Under the gate a small crowds kneelin. A tall shaved bloke in white robes stand in the middle. Praise be the Law, he say an the kneelers say, Praise be. Fear the Law yer god who see us an watch us even in our secret places. Nights no hidin place nor under any roof. Thru nights blindness the Law pierce an thru that roof under that blanket even into yer heart he look an bring judgement on you.

A stranger scamp past an Aban win him back. A bad-smellin bloke, he hold a skinned coon thats drippin blood an flies. Wassup, say Aban. That bloke there –

The coon man take our looks walk then snatch back his eyes. Jellico man, he say.

A what?

Lots of em bout these days. Where theres poor folk run from they homes the Jellicos aint far behind. Its like they got a nose for it. Like kites an crows. Where death go they follow.

Who are all these people, say Dowd.

Why, say the coon bloke. Where you from an all with yer ouster talk?

Hes cool, say Aban. Hes our mate.

Lotsa robbers got mates. The coon bloke shake a dust of flies off his meat. Come from all over, he say to Efia. Crowstorm. Fansted Riches.

Is there fightin, say Dowd.

Aint there always when the rains fail? Now scuse me I got mouths to feed.

Wait, say Efia. The Jellico man, can he help us?

The coon bloke think on this but look at Dowd all sneery. Preachers all native, he say, only care for stedders. No ouster blood in em see. No polushun.

Dowd turn from Efias look an watch the small crowd prayin. The Law mans swayin now, his face red, his arms liftin up to the arches.

Every way you look, the Jellicos sayin, an every place you go its loyal folk suffer. Its christun folk like you an me. Every way the false gods marchin. Ousters an they demon prophet. Hoofers an they black magic. An now this

Momma our girls talk about. What Momma? I ask. What demon bitch livin in the mud an forests? Aint no true gods I say just idols. Idols an lies. But they kill us good folk. They bring the Laws rage on us. Thunder an drought an sandstorm. Pox an blight an locusts. All you suffer an yer kin. Till we ask the Law to spare us as worship. Not the prophet. Not Momma with her milky dugs. The Law our Father. The Law our maker an our breaker. Turn away oh turn away yer anger from us! Fix it on our enemies that want us dead! Cut they roots an ring they bark so the tree of they people die. Dam up the rivers of they women. Smash they children like eggs on the ground. Heap they slaves like grass an set em aflame.

Best be off, say Efia. She take Abans hand an feel the stone hes carryin. That carvin flint.

Spread yer curses on they heads. Bring em pox an river blindness.

Go slow, say Dowd. Dont look rushed.

Let the wind strew they ashes in the ditch of forgettin.

Efia, say Aban.

Let beasts tramp they dust in the ground.

Efia Im sorry.

Let no sign remain of they stay on this earth.

Bout the guidin stick.

Let it go, say Efia. It dont matter alls forgot.

Thru the redwood camp an its silent people. Hungry dull eyes under fronds an trash. To the shelter where the others waitin.

No good, say Efia. Theres fightin hereabouts an folks scapin it. This aint no safe place.

On then, say Nathin who hold the guidin stick. If fightins come we best be off before the ways flood.

How, say Becca. Davys Way take us no place it just fizz out.

The roads, say Dowd. We follow the big roads.

With juntamen all over em?

I say *follow*. Not travel on.

No good, say Aban. First time he speak to all since he forget the guidin stick. Thats no good as a plan Malk. Look we trust to the suns settin. Westways innit? So we track it an keep outsight. Cos stedders wont treat us gentle.

Nor juntamen, say Becca.

Well an we cant stay here. Heave it is or might as well hand us over at the nearest sted.

Nathin look hot at Aban, his teeth showin. Malks eyes shut like hes lookin under his lids for a better plan. He find nuthin an tell all to gree. Only Nathin shake his head till Malk say, You too.

No, say Nathin. Dont trust him.

Then don't, say Efia. Dont trust Aban nor Dowd nor me. Cos we aint got no other way.

He aint fit to hold the stick.

Then I wont, say Aban. I wont hold it no more.

Nathin think on this. He look at Becca Rona Malk. Look at the guidin stick in his hand. Rightyer he say.

So the group enter the heave for the last time.

———

First bloke we meet next days not the talky kind. He grin at us tho like he know sumthin we dont. His stretchy-out arms dont greet us cos they tied to stakes in the sand.

Malk kneel next to the corse. Tho rot to bone, clothes at the ankles might hold loot. Malk poke bout in em with a stick an dig out a skin hat. Group watch him shake out the sand. Sniff it. Try it on. Good enuf, he say, for cold nights.

Wont he mind, say Becca lookin fraid at the skull.

Na, say Rona. He dont need it now.

But the bone curse –

What bone curse, Malk say an he raise the guidin stick that live now only in his an Nathins hands.

Slow we walk where we reckons west. Slings an sharpsticks ready, watchin the heave for danger.

What, say Malk. You. Dowd. Whats yer eyes for?

Dowd say, Sorry?

Look at me like I stink.

I dont.

Give me bad eye cos I take what he dont need?

You did right, say Dowd fallin back like hes fraid Malk might hurt him.

Rightyer. Bad for you I get there first.

You are welcome to the hat.

Aint for you to give ouster boy.

Dowd keep out Malks way after this. Drop back down the group to its footprints in the sand. Only Efia meet him with a smile but Dowd dont smile back.

Come dusk an the heat less we come cross a hut in the sand. Malk make the shufty click with his tongue an we all drop. Faces low, watchin the hut. Dust risin up behind the thatch. Into sight a bloke come. A boy follow with his hands full of stuff.

Lets go round em, say Aban to Malk. Malk say, Watch first.

We study the bloke an the boy with our sharpsticks close an growlin guts. Bloke all scuzzy an his beard like crits could live in it. Strong tho, his arms like yewka trunks an hands ropey an black with use. Like his boy the bloke turn all his strength to a knot of broom, usin it to sweep the flinty ground of deadwood an brush. Nathin say, Theys looper but Aban shush him.

I seen hoofers do it, he say. Preparin campment. Clear ground of spidies. Snake tracks ul show in the sand.

Whos the boy, say Rona.

Slave. Ho. Maybe his son.

Maybe his slave ho son all one, say Nathin. Loners like that often peedo.

Peedo or not we need grub. Upyer, say Malk, lets get em.

Boy see the group first an give a yelp of fear but the bloke hardly lift his head, he just keep on sweepin. Malk Nathin up first an still the bloke dont seem to mind. Malk Nathin stand waitin for him to turn or pay heed of our silly-feelin sharpsticks. Without lookin up the bloke say, Found the bone man did you? Say hey to him? Hope you dint ask him the way cos he wont remember.

Who done the killin, say Malk.

Dunno. He wont tell.

Ouster was he?

Just a bloke. We all just blokes an poor uns when the crows been peckin.

Efia look at the heave lad. Nuthin in his face, no thinks, just a hole for eatin an spittin.

What they kill him for, say Becca.

Heave bloke shrug an drop his broom. We use to find em dead an left for crits, he say. Now its carvin after an takin bits away. Have to hate deep for that. You muck about the husk after you eat a hazenut?

What for, say Becca.

What for an all?

Not enuf killin a bloke, Malk say. Kill the corse after. Take his head an no spook follow.

You know bout killin lad?

More an you.

Rightyer. We kill only whats good for eatin. An men aint too good for that.

What you kill, say Nathin.

What we need an the heave give us.

Heave dont give nuthin. Its just dumb desert.

Dont talk like that lad. Heaves like a dump for yer bad stuff. Walk it for days an you leave yer sickness there. Heave take yer rage an sorrow. Feed you too so longs you respect it. My boy here set a trap an ask the hare to give itself.

Trappin, say Malk. Aint no magic in that. Dont take respect to catch bunnies.

Well an it work for us, say the bloke. You see what happen to they as live elseways.

Efia step between Malk an the bloke. See the anger in Malks eyes, in Nathins grip on his sharpstick. Best cool things. We dont mean no bad, she say. Just tryin to get on our way.

I aint stoppin yer, say the bloke. The heave lad snuff an wipe snot on his arm.

Efia say, You live here?

Well not here, say the bloke. Not just here. All over. Bad Shot Heaves our home an we make our livin by it.

Same as us, say Becca.

Oh no. You kids what I call bingers. Just the first birds. I know drought. I know starvin what it make men do. Soon the steds ul empty grain stores gone an folks ul flock to the heave an strip it clean. All the wild grub my boy an me live by.

It aint just for you, say Nathin.

Not sayin so just sayin. Years back last once the rains fail thousands cross this land. Like ghosts. Women could as easy be men. Children like walkin corses. Dont understand the heave dont care for it cos hunger gnaw they bellies. Dint know brains in the belly did you? So it is when hungers bad enuf.

Howd you know for show famine come?

The heave bloke look at Nathin like hes sweatin piss. Howd you know you breathin?

Be dead else.

Sure as breathin famines comin. An everythin that follow.

Thats why we goin, say Becca.

Goin where sister?

Becca, say Malk, you shut yer gob.

West Cunny. Theres water there an rain in winter. Becca look fire at Malk. We aint first to think on it, she say.

Well well, say heave bloke. Malk scowl at this well well, seemin to say, What well? Might as well have a plan as not. Good luck to you kids. An now, say the bloke, we biddy good night. Nuthin to swap nuthin to say but fairy well.

Dowd Aban Becca ready to go at this but Efia cry out, Malk no!

The shout dont stop Malk Rona Nathin from jabbin they sharpsticks near the heave blokes throat. His boy seein this leap an gibber till Nathin clout him cross the face an he fall gainst the hut.

Not so fast, Malk say to the bloke who want to help his boy. Aint gonna shift us an we got empty guts to fill.

Meats all gone, the heave bloke say. We got some locust flour is all.

Well an thats a start, say Malk, an better manners.

Malk, say Efia, put the spear down.

Shut it, say Malk. Becca go in take a look what grub you can find.

Efia turn to Aban Dowd whiles Becca nod an stoop into the huts dark innards. It aint right, say Efia. Not shoppin off poor folk. But Dowd turn away, kick stone into the lands blue shadows. Aban fight a knot in his throat, his fists clench an his eyes keep off Efias like a stingin winds gainst him. Hungry, he say.

What?

We hungry an sleepy we got no other way.

Bollocks, say Efia. *Bollocks.*

Got these, say Becca comin out of the hut with sacks of flour in her hands. Theres honey too.

Biddy sit, say Malk to the heave bloke an he do like hes told, holdin the boy to his chest. Malk swallow hard an look at the sky like he sniff or taste the night comin. Since you so good an friendy I reckon we gonna stay over. Cook us some locust cakes an make us easy. Nathin. Tie em up.

No need, say the heave bloke. We aint gonna fight you.

Too right, say Malk. Do it.

Group watch, no thinks nor words sayin, as Nathin find twine in the hut an bind up the wrists of the bloke an his son. Not too tight, say Efia but Nathin ignore her an the boy cry as his twine bite.

Please, say the heave bloke. Dont hurt the boy.

Whats he to you, say Nathin.

Look you stay an take our flour but he aint no use to you an no problem neither.

Efia snatch Abans blade an go to cut the boys bonds but Nathin get in her way till Malk say, Rightyer.

Rightyer what, say Nathin.

Cut him loose, say Malk. One wrong move from him tho an its worse than rope he get.

Nathin try to take the blade off Efia but she do the freein like she cant trust him to do it right. Nathin look fire at Efia an when Malk aint seein at Malk. The heave bloke fix his boy, speak cool words to him in a private sort of talk till the boys calmer.

Whats that, say Malk, ouster words?

Nope, say heave bloke. Hes native.

Not right is he?

Not for you maybe. Right enuf for me an the life we got.

Backways I reckon, say Rona.

Hes simple is all. Simple an good.

As night fall the group rest an fix up some grub. Malk risk a fire an theres flour an honey for porridge. The heave bloke tie up outsight the hut watch Aban Dowd Becca bring firewood. Not that, he say. Dowd look at him. Deadwoods no good. Sand in pores slow the fire. Still make do an all. Use what you got.

Malk leavin the hut hear this. Aint got, he say, much of nuthin here.

Heave bloke look at Malk, suck his lip. Depend how you look it.

Look it with eyes man.

Eyes only the gate to seein. Some blokes dont even need em. See with they feelin. *Here*. Heave bloke clap a hand to his heart.

Malk snort like sands in his face. Some blokes dont need arses, he say. Shit *here*. An he point his gob with his thumb.

Most of the group laugh at this cept Malk who tell the joke an Efia who sees Malks thinkin. This poxy bloke seem to make the land work for him. Hes wise to it, for all his spooky talk. Worth milkin if we stuck on the heave for long.

Malk bide his time till its night an we sittin well fed by the embers. Then with the bloke an his boy gnawin scraps he turn to em.

So, he say, tell us. Whats the trick for shoppin this bush? How we stay on it if drought an famines come?

The blokes eyes shrink in the fire glow. Enuf light by the moon to see his scraggy hair, like its thorns an furze. Limbs dry an tough like they made of gumwood. The heave bloke seem to churn over Malks ask. Wrong way, he say, an a burr catch in his throat. Malk look at Rona an say, Give him yer jercan.

What? No.

Give it, say Malk an Rona hand the captive her water. He drink just a gulp an nod his thanks. Pass it to the boy.

You got it the wrong way, say the heave bloke. This land aint for shoppin. You dont fight or steal from it. The heave own us it feed us cos we know how to ask it.

Bollocks, say Nathin.

Aint bollocks I see it. Folk as dont know the heaves only fit for corses. Land feed you or you feed it. Aint no middle way.

Then what, say Nathin, the fucks the right way?

Respecks a start. Then lookin close up. Learn its ways.

Such as?

Well animal tracks. You thirsty you follow em an you find a waterhole. You got to learn yer patch see. Leave stones in yewka trees to mind you where water lie. Dig for it by trees as prosper in the Dry. Look in the trunks an hollows. If theres rainwater suck it up with a stem or make a sponge of dry grass.

Fine, say Dowd. But without a well you wont go far.

You manage what you got. If on the move dont drink keep walkin till thirst eat you till it rip yer gut an brain. Then drink as much as you can much as you need. Think better after. Speak better walk safer. Make nuther nightfall.

We know all this, say Aban.

But you traipsin in daytime. That dont make sense. Move slow an easy. Dont be dancin like atters in the midday sun. Surest way an cook yer brains. Listen you go slow an shady. When its hottest stir nuthin but yer shadow. Leave off sweat till sunset.

What if you aint got time for goin slow? This Rona say, the fierce look gone out of her face like shes speakin to an elder. Dangers after us we best get shiftin.

Well then, say the bloke, go nights.

Aint long enuf, say Malk. Its summer innit.

For crysake go nights when you *can*. The bloke see Nathin shake a cramp out his legs. An take salt, he say.

Salt?

Need salt same as water.

Eat salt, say Malk, an waters all you want after.

Right but what leak out in the hot aint just water but salt also. You carry salt its less weary you get an they cramps wont come so often. The heave blokes off now, he tell us how to clean cuts, how to sleep good an scape gettin sick. Leave yer waste far from where you kip, he say. You got swats for flies what bout mozzy nets?

Where we get mozzy nets?

Trade or nab em. Dont reckon thats a trouble for you lot.

Next he tell us how to get chiggers out of our skin before they lay eggs. What plants to press gainst sores from scabby mites. To catch hoppers you form a circle an close it till you drive em on a bed of coals. Eat em roasty then. Or nab locusts when they dim with the evening cool. The group listen an learn till it get so the boy lose some of his fear an sit next to Efia. The heave blokes not so easy tho. He look at these kids holdin him captive. Turn his thinks over in his head till he say, What you runnin from friends?

We aint yer friends, say Malk. An you know what from.

Thats not how you come to be as one tho is it? What you scapin from sister? The bloke ask this of Becca like he smell shes the weakest. She look fraid at Malk for his gree or sayso. He shake his head an Becca say nuthin. But Efia speak.

What yer reckon, she say. Usual shit. For us its marryin an birthin till we bust. Aint gonna live like that.

Theres worse fates, say the heave bloke lookin Efia straight in the eye. The world bein harsh an toothsome. Some reckon love for shades a fair trade.

Yeah I hear that. Mostly blokes as say it.

So you girls scapin one thing what bout you four lads?

How bout you stop askin questions, say Malk. How bout you keep that nose in its own shit eh?

The group an bloke go quiet after this. Rona yawn an set off others yawnin. Abans eyelids cant stop droopin. The last snaps of the ashes an the moons sinkin. Till soft as leaves fallin the bloke whisper, How you kids mean to get west?

We started, say Dowd, on the old road.

Which one?

Davys Way, say Rona.

Oh ah. Run out dunnit, say the bloke. It aint done for tho. Davys Way start again a few miles west of here. All the way to Silster then. Ole Roamin town that. Very ole.

Whats Roamin, say Becca.

Roamins what this land were long ago.

Like we roamin?

Dont ask me. All I know is Davys Way dont finish here. But its not safe long it. Best stay hid. What the heaves for an dont we know it.

How about trade, say Dowd.

Round these parts? Heave bloke rub his face. Dont think on trade no more. Crowstorm. Fansted Riches. We went that way half moon back.

What you find?

Corses. Only fruit as grow in season.

Efia nod at this. We see stedders, she say. Park up in grounds this big manshun.

Rightyer, say heave bloke. Militias bin busy.

Jorjes Army?

Dunno. They carry guns. Strong stuff gainst hoofer sticks an stones.

But the army, say Becca, dont it help the steds?

Help itself lass. Worse things get the better for some. Reckon the bones you see belong to a regular. Thats what they do to boys as dont follow orders.

They kill they own?

Keep the others nasty yeah.

What, say Nathin. They bones we sees some junta bloke? Why they take his ears?

Maybe not the same folk as kill him.

An you reckon, say Efia, they do that cos he say no to fightin?

Could be.

Nathin scoff at this. An he hate fightin so much why start?

Cos he aint got nuthin to lose.

Every blokes got his life to lose, say Aban.

Plus whats pricier than life, say Efia. It come out of her without her plannin an everyone stare at her in the moon glow.

Pricier than life an whats that then, say Malk.

Just sayin, say Efia. Lifes not all a bloke can lose. But her words dont click with others an the nabber move on. Slowly the group break up for sleep. Malk Rona in the hut, Nathin outsight with the guidin stick an Becca at his feet. The heave bloke say no, but they tie up the boy case he get ideas when alls sleepin.

Efia Aban curl up near the ashes. Dowd furthest off on first watch. Fixin to wake Efia when its her turn.

Efia feel a hand on her shoulder. She wake to the dark loomin of Dowds head. At first shes fraid but, Shush, he say, please. I must tell you something.

You OK?

I must tell you something. You will understand.

What? Dowd what you done? Seein his fear of others hearin, Efia take his hand an lead him like a ma her son some way into the night.

Whats yer trouble?

Its nothing bad for you I swear. Efia, he say an for a scary sec she think he might say words she cant stand from him, cant stand from any bloke cept maybe one an that she cant say even to herself. But Dowd aint struck like she reckon. In starlight and moonlight she make out tears on his cheeks.

Hey what is it?

That time I told you about the island. The island in the river where they kept me prisoner.

Yeah?

I said to you the man I escaped with gave me fish. Bad fish to eat remember? I said Ned gave me this rotty fish.

So what?

It was a lie. I ate no fish. There was none to eat not even rotted. Oh god.

You dont have to say it.

Efia –

Dont tell me!

I ate what they gave me. I was so hungry. So hungry and I wanted to live. I thought like Malk says whats pricier than life so I put it in my mouth I *chewed* it.

Efia clap her fingers on his lips, cos he close to wakin the group hes so loud. Under her skin he go quiet an she let out his breath like a moth from her grasp.

Why tell me?

Because the words push at my teeth at my tongue like if I dont speak I will sick them up.

But you dint *kill* to eat did you?

I took what he gave me.

An cos of that you here now. Our friend.

I have no friends.

Yeah you do. Me Aban Becca.

Not Malk.

An tho it aint for me to say its like yer speakin it undone the bad of it. You rid of the bad an you done good.

But if the Law sees me. You heard what the preacher man said. The Law sees *into* us.

I dont reckon the Law do you? Dowd stare at Efia like hes never had this think. Leastways the Law aint what I look to.

But things turn Efia. Deeds turn on the doer.

An you say you sorry an dont do it no more its done an the world let you be.

But I dream about it all the time.

A dreams like smoke. You wake up an the fires out.

He say nuthin to this, just stand in the hush of the heave lookin at Efia. He reach up an touch the hand shes put on his chest. Thank you, he say. You see what the others cannot.

What?

You see outside them.

Efia drop her head an take her hand from under Dowds. Shush now, she say. Say nuthin more of this.

Yes.

You sleep an I watch.

Thank you.

Dowd walk off an lie down in the shadows. The night do its low creepin over the land an after Efias watch its Abans turn an he see the day hatch its birds an light show in the east. Aban look back to check on the group an he see the empty space where the heave bloke ought to be. Fast as can be we up an Nathins cursin, Fuckin fucker, an Malk lookin grim at the cut-up twine.

The boy, say Efia. Maybe he dunnit?

How, say Nathin. I bind him up tight.

Not tight enuf, say Becca.

I reckon we go after em. Bring em back.

What for, say Aban. Whats the point?

Might tell on us, say Nathin.

I say they run cos they fraid is all. Same as we would. Malk, say Efia, what you reckon?

Malk chew on this an go to Nathin, take the guidin stick off him. He look deep at the woods dark grain. Aban find Efias eyes. She see him thinkin but no picture of it find her brain.

Dayup soon, say Malk. Nuther hotten. Best be off.

13

Blueface

It was like a dream, one of those labyrinths of haste and obstruction, with a gibbering horror fast on his heels. A wolf, or something like a wolf, was howling in the distance. He could hear faintly the shouts of men. He let the boy steer and pull him; he had little will of his own, only deep reserves of pain and humiliation to meet the branches that slashed his face. Trees threw up their black obstacles; the ground buckled and rolled at his bloodless feet. Perhaps this was planned for him, a travesty of escape, and at any moment the boy would lead him to the teeth of a trap, or into the darkest swale and let go of his hand, leaving him blind and breathless for the sport of his enemies.

The boy stopped and Marcus was forced to do likewise. They listened for sounds of pursuit. It could only be the druid, and he could not run, surely, with that blasted leg.

They were off again, the boy railing at their pace and pulling him till his shoulder sang in its socket. He meant to oblige, and tried to think sense into his obtuse and doltish limbs. They ran and kinked and stumbled in the dark. All the while death owned him. He was death's slave.

Ice broke underfoot and he felt soft and sucking earth. Water was audible before the boy pulled him into it.

'What do you think,' he said, 'you're going to drown me?'

The water ran so cold to his knees that it was like fire. He could feel the trembling insistence in the boy's hand as he led them, not to the relief of the opposite bank, but along the bed of the stream.

Marcus looked down. Starlight shimmered beneath them. He twisted his wrist free of the boy and shook off his fur gloves. Tucking the gloves in his armpit, he reached with both hands into the water. He drank and drank, scooping bitter, foul and never sufficient handfuls to his mouth. Bent over the stream, he gulped the fuel of hope. It was stronger than any magic.

The boy tugged on his arm. Marcus felt cold flesh against his skin and realised that the boy had nothing to warm his hands.

'Quickly,' the boy squealed, and Marcus put on his gloves again. He nodded and waded after him a dozen yards or so, until the cold began to numb them both and they scrambled over ice and loose gravel onto the opposite bank.

The boy was nimble and quick but Marcus could not easily follow. Three times he tripped and once fell headlong into the frosted leaves. His guide beckoned and pulled at him.

'Damn it, yes,' said Marcus. He felt for a loose branch that he might use as a weapon, but the boy gave him no opportunity: he twitched and danced until they were moving again.

Where was he being led? Marcus longed for the open: the spread of the heath and the bright star-cloth of the sky. Anything to be free of these branches.

His guide had other ideas. Marcus distinguished bright-ness but they were in heather for a hundred yards at most before thorny scrub clawed at them again. He was dragged like this from thicket to thicket, the green flames of gorse scalding his hands and face, until the decurion's legs failed him, whereupon this wild spirit that was saving his life granted them both a rest.

———

They wriggled in on hands and knees, ignoring the scratch-ing of leaves. Where the boughs touched the ground, at the heart of the holly, they would find a green door against the wind.

Going first, Andagin flushed a blackbird and winced to hear its scolding.

In the dark womb of the holly, upon its pricking bed, they sat and nursed their sorrows. Andagin did not wish to think about Judoc. Could he be on their trail? Had he captured the other soldier, or come to grief in the attempt? He scowled to own his mind; he walked it along the route he planned. He could feel the soldier watching him, saw his night-shadow crouched and fearful. He supposed it was possible that the man might hurt him. He would resist of course, but could not hope to withstand a determined assault.

Andagin's fingers no longer burned with cold. They had grown numb, thick and stupid and scarcely his. He tried not to think of the mittens he had lost. If he did, he might howl like a baby. He clenched and unclenched his fists, breathing on his knuckles.

He heard the soldier shuffle beside him. Gently, warm fingers took hold of his wrist. Andagin was afraid for a heartbeat, then felt fur against his skin.

'I cannot take these,' he said, trying to hand the gloves back, and the soldier replied in Andagin's language:

'Aye. Take them.'

'You understand me?'

'Very small.'

'I cannot take your gloves. You will need them.'

'Please.'

'I can warm my hands in my cloak,' Andagin said, and buried them there to refuse the offer. Secretly he turned the Mother's stone with his fingers, swapping it from hand to hand until his blood began to move again. He was glad of the pain, like nettle-rash: it meant he was not yet frozen. He remembered his grandfather's corpse when they brought it back from the heath. He did not want such a purple, bitter end.

'Do you,' he whispered, 'follow my words?' He could sense the warmth of the soldier, smell his rancid, thirsty breath.

'Follow some.'

'How?'

'A man. One of your men. I know at my camp.'

'One of our people?'

'He teach me.'

Not well, thought Andagin. His accent was thick and the words simple like those of a child.

'Why do you do this?' the soldier asked.

Andagin was silent. The man speaking his tongue, even badly, was unlooked-for luck. He needed the words that would carry most, and the effort made him light-headed. It was easier to run in darkness than to find his way in words. 'I help you,' Andagin said at last.

'Yes and why?'

'Because I need your help.'

There was no time to say more. They heard the baying

of the hound. Human whistles plotted movement through the scrub.

Andagin went first, scrabbling clear of the holly. The soldier followed. Their tree stood in a copse of rowan: a weft of saplings concealed them even as it slowed them down. They fought their way free and were exposed on the winter heath.

Enough old snow remained on the ground to show them up under starlight. Yes, it was easy to move, but safer to go slow and hidden. Andagin ran, stooping, towards a familiar clot of trees.

Through winter's undergrowth, the scorched fronds and juiceless brambles, they dragged their bodies.

'Where do we go?' the soldier whispered.

'Calleva Atrebatum.'

14

No Man's Land

Dust. In his nostrils. Aitch breathes it in with a snort and it rattles in his throat.

He doesn't wake, not from a night like that, not in a place like this. He gets mugged by daylight. The sun duffs him up. His bed is sand and gravel and winter grass. He moans like a bear, as if someone might take pity on him. But he is as he always will be, alone. On the chuffing heath, with the old blockhouse for a bedhead. He smells puke and it might be his or it might be the gunk inside that concrete shell.

Half ironically, he pats himself down, checks that his balls are where he left them. The cash he had in his back pocket isn't. Spent it, didn't he. Down the Three Mariners, trying to obliterate yesterday. But it didn't work. There's a bus ticket in place of his banknotes and he blinks at it to decipher a telephone number and an address, and immediately he remembers.

Three lads in the beer garden. Cocksure, more than he was at their age. One of them he knew by sight – it's his handwriting on the bus ticket. Gary Hazzard. Bekah used to shag his brother, Duke. Gary recognised Aitch, introduced him to his mates as a war hero and that didn't set him off like it should because he'd already had a skinful.

Gary must have been the oldest. Nineteen, twenty tops. Aitch can't be sure the others were even eighteen – they were fresh-faced under their grime. Where'd they been to get like that? They couldn't wait to tell him, raving about their 50cc two-stroke bikes, the laugh they'd been having on the heath, dodging the rangers and taking the piss out of old farts who tried to stop them.

Aitch admits to himself, he'd wanted to put them in their place. They spoke about their Suzukis like they were high-tech killing machines, so he gave them both barrels. How he started riding when he was ten and his dad gave him a beaten-up Yamaha TY80 and he got dented and cut up on that bike, but he loved it, the power it lent him, 40 mph while other kids laboured uphill on their BMXs. How he graduated to bigger and nastier bikes, bigger and nastier injuries. It was the usual bullshit. The lads surrounded him on the bench and it turned his head. He fended off their questions about Afghanistan, but only because it made him look harder. Stuffing his face with cheese and onion crisps, fake pork scratchings, laughing when they told him some anecdote about knocking over a birdwatcher. It was all so funny – Aitch had mates and they liked him because he was the adult who went to the bar to buy them beer.

'We're gonna ride tomorrow,' Gary said. 'You can join us if you like.'

Aitch was swaying and gurning and yeah, he said, cool, why not? And Gary Hazzard's contact details are in his grubby fingers.

He looks at the address. His head's a plundered hive, each thought a raging bee.

Water. He needs water and a lie-down and something to eat – Rachel could make it for him, but the vicarage is too far away and he could no more face her after a night on the lash than he could his sister.

Desperate measures – what choice did he have? He's a war hero, isn't he? They'll let him in. After all he was invited, and it's not as if he has anywhere else to go.

Dragging his heels, he sets off across the heath towards the Old Dean.

Her father is in her room and talking before she is fully awake. Light erupts through the curtains and she buries her face in the pillow.

'Up, up,' he says.

'*Why?*'

'Because today is a red-letter day.'

Bobbie wishes her hair were long so she could hide under it. 'I don't even know what that means.'

'A stonking day.'

'No one says stonking. Hey!' He has grabbed hold of the sheets and pulled them off her. She tugs down her nightie.

'Come along, Grumplestiltskin. I have to be gone in half an hour.'

She looks at him reproachfully, picking sleep grit from the corners of her eyes. He is dressed as yesterday for the heath. There is beard shadow on his chin. How much has he slept?

'Dad –'

'Get up!'

'Where are you going?' He stands half hidden behind the door, as if there is someone behind it tugging on his arm. 'How's your head?' she asks him.

He steps back into the room. 'My head is absolutely fine. Don't you worry about my head.'

'You've got some scheme, haven't you?'

'If that's what you want to call a perfectly coordinated law enforcement operation.'

'Dad!'

He sits on the edge of the bed, and she sees the fervour in his eyes, the fever.

'What happened yesterday was the last straw. I've been on the phone to the MoD, the rangers – they've had enough. And Surrey Police are going to throw everything they have at it. Patrol cars and air support.'

'You're not going out there again.'

'They need spotters on the ground. There hasn't been time to assemble volunteers.'

'Don't you think you should stay at home?'

'I'm not concussed.'

'I'd like you to stay.' But he does not hear. 'Please.'

'They behave as if the land belongs to them. They tear it up and burn it. And for years now, the worst they get is a police caution. These yobs are habituated lawbreakers – they're laughing at us. It's time to prosecute someone, haul one of them in front of a magistrate and see how he likes it.'

There is a rush of heat inside her. It must show in her face, a dew of panic on her upper lip. 'I really don't think you should get involved.'

At once, he is furious. 'You're being ridiculous. You're being completely unreasonable.'

'Dad, you got assaulted.'

'And that was the catalyst! You never let an opportunity like that go to waste.'

'Then,' says Bobbie, 'let me come with you.' She does not want to go; she does not want to go, but at least she has quenched his anger. It falls to her, to Bobbie, to protect him. Mum wouldn't want him going anywhere after what happened yesterday, after what's been happening to him, and inside him, for weeks. Because of his father's death. Because of the divorce. Everything he's ever loved slipping away, so that he clings to what remains. 'You need spotters on the ground,' she says. 'And there hasn't been time to round people up.' She watches him lean back, cooling even as the heat roils inside her. 'Let me come with you.'

'I'm not sure,' he says.

'We're not going to be at the sharp end, are we? I don't want to spend another day here on my own.'

She watches the battle within him between his madness and what remains of his better judgement. 'Let's have breakfast,' he says. 'We'll decide after we've eaten …'

———

Only when he gets to the path in front of the semi (ragged lawn, smashed pallets, a dying shrub) does it occur to him that he has no idea of the time. Possibly the lads will be asleep. They won't welcome him if he crashes in on their hangovers.

He looks at his watch. Nearly nine. Late for working people, early for the likes of them.

Only he's dying of thirst.

The knocker has broken off so he applies his knuckles. It's Gary Hazzard who opens, and though Aitch expects him to gawp while he ransacks his memory, he greets him with a grunt and leaves the door ajar. Inside, it's pretty much what Aitch imagined – three or four young men free at last to live like rats. He glimpses a living room and a pair of naked feet surfacing from the depths of a sofa. It all stinks of weed.

Gary Hazzard leans against the kitchen units as Aitch makes his way to the sink. The lad's in biking leathers.

The sink is a shantytown of takeaway boxes. Aitch soaks the lot as he runs the cold tap and leans under it to gulp and gasp. Water dribbles down his chin but he's not proud, it's life he's taking in, it's freshness and greenness and it fills him with joy. He surfaces to contemplate a can of wife-beater.

'Hair of the dog,' says Gary.

Aitch can't be sure if he's being made fun of. Does Gary know he's a charity case? Does he think Aitch is a pisshead like his old man?

'Na mate, cheers,' Aitch says, and without expression Gary returns the can to the fridge. 'You're all here, are you?'

'Jim is. Sandy's gone for a job interview.'

'Oh yeah?'

'Mechanic.'

'Is he?'

'Reckons he is.'

Now that he's here, Aitch hasn't the foggiest idea what to say, what these lads are to him or he to them. Gary doesn't seem fussed – he shuffles off to the living room and Aitch contemplates leaving, only that would look rum, the sort of thing a homeless drifter would do, so he goes after him and there's Jim in his boxers, belly creased as he crouches in the middle of the sofa skinning up.

Gary plonks himself on the floor next to the telly and applies himself to a hangnail. 'You up for that ride?' he asks, and Aitch isn't sure who he's talking to. Jim says nothing, so it must be him.

'Uh, sure.'

'You can borrow Sandy's wheels.'

'Yeah, why not?' The tap water has brought Aitch back from the brink. He feels fucking shit, which is an improvement. Get some scoff inside him and he might make it through another day. 'Sandy'd be all right with that, would he?'

'He won't give a toss,' pipes Jim, 'so long as he gets it back in one piece.'

'I'm good,' Aitch says, bristling. 'Been racing since before your voice broke.'

Jim pauses, the rollie half gummed in his fingers. 'I didn't mean nothing by it,' he says, and it occurs to Aitch that he's afraid of him, probably he doesn't even want that spliff, it's all for show. They're just kids acting tough.

'How's Duke these days?' he asks Gary, to take the heat out of the moment.

'Yeah, he's all right.'

'He's still racing, is he?'

'Na – got kids, wife won't let him.'

'There's a warning to us all,' Aitch says. He remembers Duke, Bekah's boyfriend when Aitch was twelve or thirteen. He and the older lads got themselves a great beast of a motocross and revved it on the road till their heads buzzed. Aitch would watch whoever tried to tame it gunning so hard into the heath he wondered if they'd make it back alive. Christ knows where the rest of those lads are now. Haulage drivers, probably. Security guards. Tabard-sporting hosts at B&Q.

Gary gets up with a squeak of biking leather and goes to the kitchen. He returns with plates and a loaf of Mighty White, a tub of margarine and some strawberry jam. Aitch doesn't wait for permission, cramming it into his gob while Jim lights up and drags smoke into his lungs. Aitch takes a toke when he hands it over – just enough to take the edge off.

Gary goes to wash his teeth and have a piss – he leaves the door open so they can hear everything – and comes back to rescue Aitch and Jim from their silence. He carries a biker's helmet, white, for main roads, which he tosses at Aitch.

'What, am I commuting?'

'Can't find Sandy's, it's all there is.'

Aitch lifts and lowers the black-tinted visor. It's a bit prissy for dirt-biking. 'I'll take it. I know the value of helmets. Seen 'em save lives in Afghan.'

He's pleased with the effect this has. They know he most likely killed people. He's harder than they can ever be. And knowing that's a buzz, isn't it? Quite the little ego trip.

She rolls the stone about in her pocket. Her talisman. Its ridges fit into the rounded flesh beneath her thumb. Its parallel furrows are like the concentric whorls of a fingerprint.

She lifts the stone out of the pocket and swings her arms with it nestling in her fist.

The heath is blazing hot already as Bobbie and her father reach the summit of the hill. She sees him repeatedly check his phone for a signal, but it proves unnecessary. The forest ranger – a grossly obese man, not the tanned athlete Bobbie was expecting – meets them at the western barrier of the Poors and hands over a walkie-talkie.

'Mike,' says her father. 'This is my daughter.'

'Hello,' says the ranger, and he gives her a wink as if she were a little child. She dislikes the man instantly. 'The MoD Land Rover is stationed north of Barossa. Chopper's on the way from Guildford. Better hope we catch someone after all this.'

Her father acts strangely with the ranger. It's embarrassing to see him roll his shoulders and swagger like a cowboy. Bobbie wanders off while Mike talks him through the comms protocol. She peers down the gravel firebreak that runs to the telecoms tower. Her stomach is a cold hollow. She can think only of her mother, where she might be at this instant, what she might be doing. She ambles back to her father and Mike, who is saying, 'No heroics, please. These are feral kids we're dealing with.'

'You don't have to tell me.'

Mike wishes them luck and waddles to his idling four-by-four. 'You'd have to fancy your chances,' says Bobbie, 'outrunning him when he's not behind the wheel.'

'Now, now,' her father says, but she's glad to see him smile. 'We're to stay here, you understand. Block off the escape route through the Poors.'

'Shouldn't we hide or something?'

'Would you like to hide?'

'Gets out of the sun at least.'

'Why not? Make an adventure of it.'

Parallel to the firebreak, and marking the limits of the Poors, the gorse grows tall and dense. They edge into it, finding a hollow just large enough to crouch in.

Far away in the Old Dean estate, there is a blast of noise. Two-stroke engines. Like the blorting of ancient war horns.

Their eyes and thoughts tangle. She sees him reach for the walkie-talkie in his pocket.

Her father stands up to watch the access road that separates the Poors from army training land. Nothing yet, though both can hear the engines. A minute. Another.

Two bikers roar past their hiding place. Through gorse needles Bobbie sees dust and the speeding helmets, one blue and one white.

Her father is on his walkie-talkie. 'It's Richard Borowski. Two bikers heading your way ... Will do.' He crouches to speak to her. 'Do you want to know the tactics?'

'Get cramp?'

'So we're setting a trap. Mike is stationed on the Devil's Highway west of Star Point, the MoD blocks the eastern exit. Meanwhile the police guard the gate back to the housing estate. The bikers won't be able to escape along the Devil's Highway, so they'll come back south, and if they try to make a break for it through the heath, we have, I have, to dissuade them.'

'How do you plan to do that?'

'Stand in their way. The helicopter will be driving them towards the officers on the ground.'

'Do they know I'm here?'

'Who?'

'The police.'

Her father's eyes are big and bright like he's on something. His mouth is wet. 'You're not,' he says, 'to do anything. This is my job and you stay hidden.'

'But –'

'We're just a cog in this operation. We don't try to stop them or make an arrest. We just block off an escape route.'

'What if they ride straight at you?'

'They won't try anything with a police helicopter over their heads. It'll be like herding sheep.'

'Right.'

'Really angry sheep.' He bleats and makes a furious face and Bobbie is good enough to simper at it. He puts the walkie-talkie on low volume and stows it in his trouser pocket.

They crouch in the prickly shade. Bobbie's stone is hot from the heat of her flesh.

They wait.

15

The Heave

The day dont give itself to walkin. Groups just off when the sun turn brown like a rotty fruit, like it burn itself out an trees start to shake, dust start to bite. We hear the howlin first. Scowl into the wind till we see it buildin. Risin up fast, a wall of sand an bush, scraps churnin an boilin cross the heave. Bracin for the shock we ball on our knees as the wave smash over us. Like we could drown it come racin up, yankin hair an stabbin eyes an lips. Force each on us to shrink into our lonesum. Tho others near each ones alone. Till Efia feel hands grip her hood an Abans in her face yellin, Hold me, an she catch the crumbs of his words before the wind snatch em away. So she grab Aban an find other hands closin in. Becca, now Dowd is it, an someone else grippin her foot. This go on, each scuttlin to find others till as one the group anchor down gainst the wind. In anger it throw stuff at us, a thornbush, some planks, a scythe of flyin metal. A dead bird pin itself to Dowds back an all hear him screechin like its Davy his self lay a hand on him. Efia see Dowd reach for the corse an throw it into the wind. Then a blow knock her over.

Like nightfall the air go dark, she fold into a roar so loud theres no space to hear herself cry. Keep a hold on her thinks then. Remember shes Efia, this is Aban, these are Malk Becca Rona Nathin Dowd. Picture the group to bind her thinks to it cos elseways this storm drive her mad. Try to breathe low to the ground, make a burrow of air with her body. Mouth shut, nostrils burnin. A mass of bodies holdin fast to life. Waitin for the horror to blow over cos it dont care if we live or die. Dont need witnesses. Just the world ragin like the world must. Till the rage wear itself out or take itself elseways. Into places we scape from for ever.

Who can say how long the storm last, it get so our legs numb, our thinks blank an gobs gum up with dry spit. Malk hide in sleep cos when the blast ease Nathin podge him an Malk snort an say, Wha?

Malk, say Nathin, his voice dusty an broke. The storms passin where we go what we do?

Malk nod then slap the back of his head like to wake him. Blinkin at the sand ghosts before us. Dowd spittin or tryin to spit, Becca whimperin, Aban Efia pickin grit out each others eyes.

War, croak Malk.

Eh?

Water.

Nathin shift fast an give Malk his jercan. Malk pull like a billykid on its mammys tit till others feel likeways an its all guzzlin with no thinks for after. Wind still raw but not so bad we cant rise up an kick blood into our legs, feel it come stingin back. Shake the sand off our clothes, scan the horizon. The scrubs gone white an trees bent like they lookin at the storm tide driftin up they trunks. Nuthin doin but walk on, make ground an look for shelter. Go slow. Head west. Into the ache of empty bellies. Like hungers got our guts on a spool an its drawin us in till we stop to stop it. Gnawin grub from our backpacks, eyes searchin the heave for food or trouble.

Efias up first lookin thru the packs. Frettin, say Nathin but she flip him a finger an line up the jercans. Only one still full. Grub not much better when we finish what we start.

Soon as we can we up an off. Sky clear now an the sun howlin at us. Poundin skulls an eyes. Like a beast ridin our backs it dig its toes behind our knees, weigh down our hips, gnaw our necks. Till we bow under it. Each step a battle. Sweat mixin with sand to streak our skins. Each thinkin we never feel such heat in all our days. Like the suns tumblin inwards or the worlds fallin sunways. Hurtlin into that ragin ball.

There.

What?

Look, say Rona. Aint that smoke?

Bushfire, say Aban.

No. Its cookin.

Best be off, say Becca.

An nuthin to eat or drink? Lets check it, say Aban an he look to Malk who hold the guidin stick. Malk nod an lift the stick.

We chase the smoke to its fire root.

What we finds no stedders up for trade but black ruins. The smoulderin ribs of huts. Bust-up tents an a twitchin dog. Lookin sharp we search for a well. Hopin ones not broke or worse.

Hard to make out much at first. Fire an sand leave a wrack of dust an ashes. Broke stuff mostly. A roastin smell find us an lead to a bloke in the beams of his hut. Arms out like the muscles still at work an fists clenchin. Flesh black charcoal. Head with its pain still showin. From out his

belly guts swell like fat grubs. On the hut step the scorch
marks of a cookin fire, only yards from the corse. Becca
sift the ground for left beans an corn.

Aban kiss the pray patches on his curta an others do
likeways. Keep the evil off us. Goin from ruin to ruin an
findin only the dead.

How long you reckon?

Malk look at Efia who ask the question.

Fresh, he say. One day or two.

Are you not angry, say Dowd.

Gainst who?

The men who did this.

Hoofers, say Nathin with a shrug.

Can you be sure?

Hoofers dont belong no place dont respect em as does.
Tramp grass with they goats an leave folk as belong nuthin
but desert.

Hoofers, say Rona, all ousters. An stink at that with
they ouster grub an lingo.

Rightyer, say Nathin. You ever hear hoofer speak right?
Hoofers make nuthin. Dont grow grain dont deserve to eat
least not at spence of folk as work the land.

Oh I see, say Dowd an Efia can see hes tremblin. Like
you lot I suppose.

Born here thats us. Nathin stab the point of his sharpstick in the sand between Dowds feet. Dowd look at him
like he mean to fight for it so Efia say, There aint nuthin
here for likes on us lets go.

Us, say Nathin. An whos that then? Nuthin to eat nor
drink an we got to drag this ouster with us?

Nathin, say Malk. Thats enuf. Efias right. We find water
or best be off.

Long search turn up a well an Aban push off the lid.
Out rush a stream of flies. We see no sky in the waters

mirror. Only a stink of rotty flesh. Bastards, shout Rona. Sicko bastards!

No water in our guts, we hide from the sun in a hot womb of thorns. Waitin out the hottest with Becca startin up, Why? Why kill an burn what you cant eat or carry?

Why not, say Aban. Flames easy to start an hard to stop. Keep burnin then. Hope yer fire beat the others fire tho fire aint got no sides just hunger an all it want to eat.

Water stem fire, Efia say.

Nathin Becca Rona holler, Where you find water if you far from a well?

Sand do as good, say Efia. Aban look at her an she feel a burnin not like fire in her throat. Aban smile his tidy smile the group can see but the bright in his eyes just for Efia.

Sand can work, he say. Stop fire easy.

How you lift enuf, say Nathin. How you scoop enuf to stem the fire? Tell us Aban an you know so much.

Just sayin, Aban say. Anyways its killin we speakin of. Fire just a way for talkin closer to it.

If fire mean killin, Malk say, how you stem that?

Aban flap his lips an Efia see the muscles in his jaw. Dunno the word, Aban say. Dunno the word but it stem fire better than water.

Love, say Efia.

The words a bird that fly out from a bush. Rona Becca dang they gobs an Nathin Malk stare. Becca laugh first. Love for shade, she say. Love for shades a good trade.

No, say Efia.

Love for shade! A good trade!

Not that, say Efia. Not grindin. But Rona Becca Nathin laughin now, they got they chant like kiddies a ball they toss between em. Only Malk in his way an Aban Dowd keep out of it. Malk standin with the guidin stick, holdin it not right way but like a spear or club. Eyes down in the far-off dust.

Efia see him rise. Stiffness takin every muscle. Malks face like a hand strike it. Thru the song an laughin Efia feel cold panic. Malk, she say. Wassup?

All the group hear the shake in Efias voice an the laughter die. Bodies stiff in that cage of thorns we strain to see out. Becca whimper, tho shes the last to know whats headin our way.

Men. Twenty or more with packs an camels, wadin out of the heat pool. Lopin like dogs. Wakin dust with they boots. Some carry clubs an sticks. Mashtis hangin like sharp fruit from they wrists. Others with guns strap to they backs. Akays an autos. Headin for the ruins till no more than a spears throw from our hidey place.

Best be off, say Becca, best be *off* –

Shush.

Malk crouch low an all do likeways. Thorns hide us an theres nuthin worth pickin over in the scrub.

Only the men got a hound on a lead.

It smell us for show, say Rona. We gotta run.

Who hold the guidin stick? *Me*, say Malk. Cant go thru that but give us away.

God oh god, say Becca.

So we wait for em to sniff us out?

Shut it *all* on you.

We turn quiet cos the men close now. Kickin down the huts, stabbin the ashes with they sticks. Voices cheery like its not a bone ground. The blokes dont have uniforms, only scraps an rags. Bits of combat cammo. Two wearin helmets. One sign mark em all. On shirts an sleeves, a white stickman with hoe in one hand mashti in the other.

Juntamen, say Aban.

The whole group feel sick. Never so awake in years. Every thorn an flint solid an the carder song like its fizzin in our heads. Deaths come callin. A dog bark an its here.

Dowd look cross the thorns to Efia. His face. His lips tight an sweat all over em. Her own face a mask of wet an guts churnin to stew.

Listen, say Dowd. When I run you break for it. Go as fast as you can. I will lead them off.

Dowd *no*.

They will find us. They find us and its over.

Stay, say Efia.

But Dowds risin. Fucks sake run, he say. *Run*.

Like in a dream we watch him crash thru thornbush. Tearin him on its claws, arms up gainst his face like a bloke runnin into flames. For a sec or two hes slow cos of the furzes grip, then hes out in the open an hes runnin fast away from the guns.

Quick, say Malk as the huntin dog wake its bark an its gainst different thorns hes pushin, Efia fast after an Aban Rona Becca Nathin. Brush catchin what it can an nuthin doin but take each lash tho worse than thorns the noise we makin. Only the blokes shouts an the dogs coughin cover us. Malk beat off the last branches with the guidin stick. Blood from torn lips in our mouths. Eyes scaldin, heads like a cloud of mozzies.

Crack of gunfire. Efia cry out, *Dowd*, an she try to turn back. Aban block her. More shots an Efia jerk like shes hit an No, shes screamin, fightin Aban till she cant win an then hes tryin to prop her up but its like keepin sand from fallin an all the others watch just burstin to be gone.

Efia we must go. We must.

Shouts cross the brush still an the dogs barkin like hes sayin, *Heres more on em*. Efia, say Aban till hes on his knees in the dust an lookin up he see Nathin run cross open ground to a kaysha wood an Malk Rona Becca caught between till its too much for Becca an shes after Nathin an then Rona give in leavin Malk with his useless guidin stick.

Abans eyes cling to Malk. Efia dead weight in his arms. Then crashin sounds thru scrub behind us an Malk break from Aban. Snappin the bond of they eyes hes off cross the heave to join the others.

Aban look weepin at Efia. Please, he say. Let me live. An its like sumthin start up again inside her. Her head in his shade. His thinks find hers an plant a word there. The word she speak before. What stem fire better than water.

He stand an her hand go after. Up like a bird for him to catch. The strength in his arm pulse thru her. Two sets of muscles grip an Efia find her feet. Calls of men comin thru the thorns but its too sharp for em to hurry. Givin Aban an Efia time to get away.

16

Blueface

The native boy stopped ahead of him. Marcus was glad of the chance to catch his breath.

'Do you hear?' The whites of the boy's eyes gleamed in the dark.

'What is it?'

'Quiet.'

'I can't help breathing.'

'They are gone.'

Marcus sieved the night noises for sounds of pursuit. Only the breeze in the branches. Perhaps Glyco was still out there. Perhaps he had turned on them and the conspirators lay dead in the heather. That would make Glyco a legend in the forces and he, Marcus, its shameful secret: the officer dragged to safety by a stripling. If they made it. If Glyco still lived.

'Follow,' said the boy.

They crawled and stooped beyond the clutch of branches, into the snow. 'We move faster,' the boy said and spoke rapid words that Marcus did not understand.

'Wait – wait. How do you know the way?'

The boy considered the question. He turned on his heel,

his head tipped back and his mouth agog. 'There,' he said. 'Like this.' He made a V shape with his index fingers. 'It is the flight of geese. That is south. So there –' He turned again and pointed at stars that Marcus knew: the Seven Plough Oxen with the steadfast star above them. 'That,' said the boy, 'is north.'

'To the road?'

'Yes.'

'We follow the *road*?'

Again the boy spoke too fast. It was wearying. Without the step-by-step absorption of trying to move in darkness, lassitude spread like fever through Marcus's body.

His guide seemed to have no such difficulties. Like a kid goat he skittered off into the heather and Marcus had no choice but to follow. Dense swells of ling required them to wade like fishermen in shallows. Each stride plunged needles into Marcus's lumbar, for the cold and his immobility in the grove had wounded him. Perhaps sensing this, the boy was careful to guide them onto fresh browsing, where fires had left only low growth and the brittle charcoal of burned stems.

He was steered thus, pulled and cajoled, south of the native settlement: close enough to distinguish the hill fort against the sky. Perhaps they both had enemies in that place of darkness. It would have to answer for what had been done to him.

They walked together in silence beneath the stars. Soon it was all heath and emptiness again. Marcus had no sense of direction. Were they level with, or beyond, the place of ambush? He had no wish to encounter what remained of Lucius and Celer and the horses.

He felt his legs fail him. The boy leapt to help but was too late.

'I must sleep. Damn it, I don't know the word – *sleep*.'

The boy shook his head. 'I have been injured and starved, I can go no further.'

The boy made a despairing gesture and watched him where he sat.

Marcus contemplated the frozen heather. A dream pressed down on his head. He fought it with a jerk and groaned as needles of pain swept through his neck.

'Yes,' said the boy. 'Yes, follow.'

'Enough follow.'

'Not here. Come.'

Marcus crawled like a baby onto his hands and knees. He growled as he concentrated all his efforts on standing up. There. First task done.

The boy led him slowly across the sleeping earth.

'Oh, no more thornbushes,' said Marcus, but his helper seemed to know the place: a clot of gorse into which sheep had gouged a cavity with their bodies. Marcus slumped among the tufts of thorn-carded wool. 'Wait, where are you going? Don't leave me!'

The boy returned and made a gesture of lifting food to his lips. He patted Marcus on the chest as if he were a pet dog in need of comforting. Then he was gone for a long time.

Marcus closed his eyes; he breathed like a bellows and sleep, which he craved, kept its distance. He prayed for it but his mind had other intentions. It travelled back to his childhood hills – the drifting cloud shadows, the wheat in its summer burnish, the wheeling and screaming of swifts. His remains would never make it home. The insurgents wanted to rob his soul as well as his life. To trap it for ever as an offering to their idols. Had he such a thing to lose: an essence that survived death? If so, could it rise from any bonds that earth could make for it? His enemies, every one of them, had a soul. The young fanatics chasing him: so long as he could stand and manage a stick, he would not hesitate to kill any that came his way. There would be no honour in it: they were not worthy adversaries. Yet the druid had found a calling for them, an exalted purpose. Who, in their stultified tribe, had done the same? Only violence stirred the blood. It was a spring that never ran dry. Perhaps that was why the empire existed, pushing ever outwards to keep the rage of its young men from turning against home.

He must have slept for a while, for he cried out with fear as a body scrabbled towards him.

It was the boy. He extracted from his pack a few sprigs of elderberry, some hips and haws and bitter crabs. Marcus grimaced like a cat with a chicken bone to strip the flesh from the stems. The food was hateful to chew. Side by side they ate and spat and rested.

The boy was quiet, sullen with unspoken words. This made Marcus voluble, for he feared despondency in this child whose purpose kept them alive.

'Have you ever eaten a grape? Figs?' He was not understood. He hoped that his tone, at least, might communicate to the boy. 'Where I come from, there are fruits you have not dreamed of. And great plains of wheat, sweeping as far as the eye can see.'

The boy looked at him without comprehension.

'Do you like to hunt? I should have asked the word of Condatis. Animals.' He said the last word in the native tongue. 'There is good hunting in Tuscany. Do you like to …' He made a dumbshow of tracking and spearing and skinning game. Yes: the Briton seemed to understand, and together they mimed in the gloom. Marcus felt the boy revive. Here was a brave lad; perhaps he might find a role for him, if they made it to safety.

The boy was talking quickly, something impossible to follow about gifts. 'You, Romani. You take.'

'If it is there for the taking.' He tried to marshal the native words at his command. How to explain sacrifice and its rewards? Hard work and wages? He knew that the natives did not own land privately but held it in common. No wonder they had little appetite to build in stone and leave their mark. These people used wood and mud. Their memory was like the black wax of a tablet with no stylus to reveal the light beneath. That was Rome's mission. They were giving these barbarians the gift of history.

'I know,' he said, 'why your people fear the road. You find your way by it – only you do not *want* to find your way. I mean directly. You want to weave and stumble and turn about.' He could hear the boy breathing. A child of the wild tangle. 'We build roads to own the land, to make it ours. And you need them to sell your wares. To buy your ingots of iron, your salt. You need our peace. We bring you these things yet you despise us.'

The boy said nothing. He sat with a coiled energy.

'Why did they hold *you* prisoner? Why –?' Marcus acted the bondage of rope and pointed at him, shrugging. 'Are they your brothers? Your people?' The boy shook his head. '*Not* your people? Another? Who are you to the bad men?'

'No, no.'

'We are friends. You say.'

'You *help*.'

'Help me, yes. But why?'

'Your king. You will let me speak to him.'

'I have no king.'

'The one with the red feathers.'

Marcus tried to imagine it: this puny lad standing up to Aulus Pomponius Capito. 'And what would you say to my king?'

'Pax.'

Marcus stared at him.

The boy spoke slowly as if to make himself understood. 'For my people. I spared you. You spare them.'

So that was it. A gamble. A plea for mercy. Well, it might not be impossible. There would be baying for blood louder than a dozen hounds, yet if he pleaded – if he spoke, with Condatis to translate, the case of this brave lad. Perhaps. The road into the future was not yet built.

'I try,' said Marcus as he reached for the boy's hand. Something hard, made of stone, lay in that trembling fist. 'Peace,' he said.

They buried the pith and seeds of their meal under the fallen needles. The boy waited while Marcus, like a shrunken colossus unsure of its strength, tested the weight of his limbs.

They resumed their journey.

It was as if dawn would never come. The boy was always before him and Marcus dragged himself after, suffering at every step. His feet were blistered, his back scourged with spasms; pain had built a nest in the swollen wound of his face. He forgot, for long periods at a time, that they were in flight for their lives. There was only the heath and his body's burden, as if the past until tonight had been a dream and he was awake in his true life, which was and always would be this ordeal in darkness, these wastes and snows, and his pain like the tribute of a slave to its master.

They came to a river which the boy called Black Water. Each knew they could not endure the cold if they tried to ford it. The boy left Marcus propped against a leaning willow, then returned with hope in his step. He had found a bridge of fallen trees, which Marcus hauled himself across, whimpering as the alders scratched his skin and dignity.

From the north bank of Black Water they walked perhaps a mile until they came to the road.

Marcus stamped on the paving. No scrub to claw their faces, no tick-infested heather to snarl up their steps. Their path was clear, the road empty. When dawn came, there would be riders, oxen and carts, the busyness of civilisation. He almost wept to think of it.

The going was good but the boy seemed uneasy. Twice, at noises only he heard, he chivvied Marcus after him into the roadside scrub. They lay there, scanning the empty sweep of the stones, then shook off the frost and frozen leaves to resume their journey. No words passed between them. Each was swaddled in his own thoughts. They found a rhythm and kept to it. Marcus had known the like many times when marching. The yielding to a greater motion; a willing servitude, with no task save to place one foot in front of the other and so continue until movement ceased.

He was in this marching daze beyond fatigue, a kind of enchantment, when messengers of light raced along the road. The frost shone like a seam of gold. He turned a weary gaze to the east, where the sun skulked on the horizon.

They were almost home. He could see orchards.

The ambush revealed itself.

'No!' cried the boy as out they came, two with slings and one – the brute – swinging a club.

Marcus shed his heaviness. He ran with the fury of hope. The boy ran too, shimmying and duping one of the conspirators. Marcus was not so agile. He bent, like a bull at charge, into the young man's body, knocking the breath out of it. He caught the side of the rebel's jaw with his fist and triumphed to see him fall.

They were still running, the ramparts of the fort visible now. Marcus felt the wind of a club swung at his head. A stone struck the paving inches from the boy. He charged, crying out in hope of alerting the sentries. Another stone whistled close. He spun about to see the tall youth wrestling with the sling-bearer, as if trying to disarm him. He ran on, and when he looked a second time the youth he had struck was on his tail again, leather strap swirling.

Marcus saw the redhead spasm after his throw.

The child, yards ahead of him, fell without a sound. He had not tripped. The projectile skittered beyond him in the road.

A trumpet sounded on the battlements. Marcus was level with the child; he meant to help him, but the redhead was armed again and sprinting to close the distance between them.

A stone tore into his shoulder. He cried out in pain and indignation, but his feet and balance were sure. He sprinted, a furnace in his chest, until the gates of Calleva were opening ...

... and infantrymen, hastily armed, were spilling out ...

... and strong arms dragged him inside and he was sinking far, far into the deep waters of unknowing ...

... and the great armoured mechanism of retribution set to work while he slept, a retribution of which he would know nothing until it was sated, though had he been conscious he could not have stopped it, the pleas for mercy of a disgraced decurion counting for little when the peace and prosperity of an empire were at stake.

17

No Man's Land

He'd almost forgotten this – if forgetting is the same as not thinking about something. As soon as he got on the saddle and revved the Suzuki to warm her up, it all came back. The reek of exhaust, the power, even of a 50cc, under his control.

It's only him and Gary – Jim didn't fancy it, too stoned or too chicken – and Gary is sound. He's got a better bike, yet Aitch reckons he has the edge when it comes to experience. Even now, his knees know how to handle a camber, he can lean into a turn, giving it throttle whenever he slides on the gravel. There are no blind corners to pit himself against – it's easy, and that's OK. He's flying. He's only half attached to the Earth.

They race north, through heath and pines, under greening beeches, in and out of shadow. Up to the big crossroads where all paths and firebreaks meet. There, Gary tacks west and Aitch follows – and instantly he sees the green Land Rover and some fatso flagging him down, and he reckons he can get around him, but the car is sideways on and the guy's built like a brick shithouse.

Gary performs a clumsy, skidding turn and Aitch turns likewise, making a tighter job of it.

East of the crossroads, they realise what they are in for. It's a shock, seeing a British Army Snatch on home soil.

Ambush. He can't believe it, the bad flaming luck. On the other hand, if they reckon they're going to catch him, they've no idea who they're dealing with.

Gary whines past as the army Land Rover rumbles Aitch's way. He watches the soldier coming on. Maybe he could wait and talk to him. One of his own. But he thinks better of it. He's not a soldier now, just a scrot on a dirt-bike.

Aitch pivots and speeds down the firebreak, back the way he came.

———

The bikers must have seen the rangers on the Roman road. Their noise clarifies and Bobbie guesses that the pair have separated, for all she can hear is the belch of one engine.

She spies a white dot above the gorse.

The biker tears past the entrance to the bridle path. Bobbie has two seconds to take in the T-shirt and the black visor. 'He's heading straight for the police,' she cries.

Her father rises from his crouching position and Bobbie does the same. Something is niggling at her eardrums. The air pulses, and above the treeline a circular blur becomes the whirring blades of a helicopter.

'Here comes the cavalry,' her father shouts.

The helicopter crowns the pines, then swoops low, nosing the heath as if following a scent. It guns towards them, a roaring dragon, then lists south in pursuit of the biker.

———

He cannot believe the chopper. Why would they go to such lengths for two guys having a laugh? He knows the bylaws, and part of him wouldn't care if they pressed charges – what has he got to lose? But another part of him is enraged. Holy fucking fury, how dare they hunt him down like a criminal on the run?

Gary has vanished – it's just Aitch and his wits. Skimming past the railing to the Poors, he checks out that option and spots him easily – a dicker in the gorse. Not exactly subtle, with his Aussie hat and binoculars.

He keeps going towards the Old Dean. Odds are they'll be waiting for him at the entrance. So he slows down and leans out to turn his head.

The two Land Rovers are coming after him. Their tactic's so obvious it's almost insulting. Gary must have gone cross-country – he'll do likewise. One dicker on stag is no obstacle if he goes at him fast.

He hurtles towards the oncoming Snatch, then veers right – a grit-spilling skid. The bloke in the hat sees him and ducks behind the gorse. It's enough to make Aitch laugh, even though the chopper is bearing down on him, the rotors echoing in his guts.

He clambers off the bike, tucks it sideways under the barrier pole, gets back on. Where's your hangover now, Aitch? He revs, just for the noise and stink of it. Off he goes, across the Poors where he once was king.

'In,' he says, 'get down.'

Her father bustles and chivvies her deeper into the gorse, then runs towards the footpath.

Bobbie can hear the bike's engine idling. She stands on tiptoe amid the thorns.

The biker is back on his saddle. He waits at the entrance to the Poors, one leg out to support his machine. The helmet and visor make him inhuman, insect. He cannot see Bobbie, only her father where he stands, arms crossed over his chest, in the middle of the footpath. The helicopter pivots above the stand-off. The biker looks up several times and appears, from the clenching in his upper body, to be cursing it.

'Come on!' Her father is shouting: 'Come on, let's have you!'

The biker goads his engine.

He's going for it!

Bobbie scalds herself on gorse as she fights it, but the thorns let her go abruptly and she falls into the heather, her cheeks pelted by grit from the bike's retreating treads. She sees Dad hold his ground, too surprised or afraid to move, and the biker careens off the track to avoid a collision. Bobbie watches the bike bounce and jolt over uneven ground, rodeo-jumping through old growth. The rider is tearing the ling but it retaliates, for however much he bucks and kicks and wrings his handlebars, he is losing momentum.

Bobbie lies in the heather while the helicopter rips up the sky. Her hand's emptiness rings in her mind. She realises that she has let go of her stone.

Her father is running and the biker has stalled. He kicks at his pedal, then flips them two fingers. Bobbie sees her father yell – or could it be a laugh? – whereupon the engine comes back to life and the biker, instead of taking the opportunity to escape off-road, performs a shredding turn in the heather.

He looks over his shoulder. There's someone on the ground. He didn't hit them. So there's that.

Only one way out. Down the hill, through the trees, behind the tower. Get back to Gary's. Dump the bike behind the bins, make a run for it to his sister's. Only the dicker's coming at him and there's the fat ranger at the barrier. He feels them closing in. The breath roars in his helmet – the darkness inside is a trap – and all the time that fucking chopper, buzzing and goading him like they reckon he's livestock for rounding up.

He gives the civilian two fingers. Kicks at the bike. Kicks and kicks – and the ugly beast wakes up under him – roars! He feels the engine in his groin and belly, and the chopper's trying to part him from it, wants him to cringe and surrender.

That's what they want him to do. So he rides. He fucking rides.

Bobbie tries to pick herself up. She sees the biker hunch his shoulders and, in a haze of exhaust, speed towards Dad.

Her father stops running – retreats – only his heel wobbles on a stone and he falls on his arse as the bike fills the space where he was standing.

Bobbie's legs are dead flesh beneath her but she pushes against the earth because her father is on the ground and searching for something, and the biker has turned yet again, and they and the biker are caught in the gale, the storm-dome of the helicopter's blades.

The motorbike roars and fumes. It tears towards Dad – is upon him – but Dad rolls over on his knees and rises and his body spasms after it.

Bobbie thinks for an instant that a bird is flying. It casts off her father's wrist like a hawk.

He has thrown something.

It is as if the biker has snagged a tripwire, or encountered an invisible branch. He tumbles backwards off his saddle, and the bike continues, appearing to accelerate for an instant, like a horse relieved of its rider, before mindlessly it wobbles, lists and falls.

Bobbie runs.

The biker is writhing on his back in the heather, his face hidden by the helmet. 'Cunt,' he shouts, '*cunt.*'

Her father is holding a stone – it's a flint, big and grey and blunt – and he lifts the stone above his head and brings it down several times in the middle of the biker's chest. Bobbie feels the impact in her own body, but the only sound is from the helicopter blades.

The biker stops writhing. Her father sits beside him in the heather.

In the corner of Bobbie's vision, the wheels of the dirtbike continue to spin.

Here's the ranger, look, trying to run!

Her father lifts his face to the sun, the stone fallen from his fist, and waits for the ranger to reach them.

18

The Heave

Aban look at Efia. Theres a picture in his head he want to put in hers. How he an she are like water drops on waste ground wantin to join the river they left, only the world wont let em. But he cant find a way into her head. Down in the ditch where they stop, heavin hot air into they lungs, Aban reach in his backpack an lend his jercan. For a sec its like she dont see it but he shake it an the water slosh reach her.

Have some.

She shake her head.

Efia we got to get back. Drink an we go after.

We lost em.

Malk ul find us.

He wont be lookin. Him an Nathin take the girls to West Cunny. He dont want us back I reckon.

Aban stare at her then at his jercan. You thirsty is all. Thirsty thinks aint straight thinks. Drink an it come right.

So Efia drink. But it dont come right. Nuther hour till dusk, she say. Best find a hidey place. More blokes patrollin herebouts.

No more sayin, she up an he after. Crouchin thru scrub

an dead grasses. Lookin till we find a ruin in the brush. Aban check it out for trouble. Nuthin home save spidies an dirt. So in we go for the night. Aban an Efia. Facin the heave on our lonesum.

———————

Next day we push on. Clingin to dark an scrubby places an watchin the roads. Far off the Thirstys got a dust cloud over it. Crowds there haulin pots, sacks, cookin oil, whatever grub they got. Fleein the dangers back east. Filin past sentries an givin up whatever juntamen fancy off they backs.

Aban Efia wont join that traffic. So we act on the heave blokes teachin. Catchin locusts at nightfall. Lookin for the heaps sand crickets make an diggin up they grubs. Keepin shady when the air quake. Hidin from the suns great hammer. Worst times it get so its hard to breathe. Like yer lungs might fry. So you stop yer thinks, you take sips of air while the other watch shadows hard as iron. Wait for carder song to hush an birds to sing the all-clear. Then Efia sit with Aban watchin the land in the softer light. She like the way it look wash clean at days end. Like the comin night could start the whole world over.

Aban let her watch him carvin his flint. She dont ask what hes doin, just like to see his brown fingers turn the blade. The cords an ropes under his skin, the nimble way he move his hands. The flints well done now, she can see its rings an dots when he put it to his lips to blow off the carvin dust.

Aban put the flint down like its heavy an sit for a long bit.

Efia.

Yeah?

Dint the trapper say Davys Way aint done?

He reckon it start again.

To Silster?

To Silster.

Maybe Malk think on the same. Maybe they gone back to look for us.

Efia turn on him like some crit bit her. You wanna find that ole road? Like it done so good for us. What *for* Aban?

For Malk.

Hes gone.

Not Malk.

Gone.

Dont say that you cant say that.

I can. Aban we aint got nobody but us.

Have to find em. Have to get back. Groups the safest place. We cant do it lonesum.

Maybe.

No. In the dark you far from people. Thats when you group. Groupins better any fire its better than a straw bed. Groups where you live when all bout yous black an toothsome.

I wanna hear –

What?

Wanna hear bout you. Not bout Malk or the group but what you seen an done before.

Before what?

Before you come a slave. What its like to be you.

He stare at her. Tho its dark in the trees theres a point of light in each of his eyes. Nuthin come out of him so Efia speak in his place.

My name mean born Friday. You dint know that did you? Lan an me we come up in the same place. Roil Wells. Dads a potter. I use to sit on his lap watchin the wheel spin. Mum help him some days. Typhus carry her off an

Dad go all stony after that. No more laughs. No more games. Just him workin an me like a slave. When my bleedin come he set me up to marry his mate. Lan too get given up for hitchin. Her name mean orchid which is a flower. We scape the town one Laws day when our dads prayin. Meet Rona an Nathin at Whey Bitch. You an Malk later.

I dint know yer name mean sumthin.

What bout you?

Dunno. Cant say.

Aban look at the flint on the ground before him. Long quiet sit between us. Then Efia say, Dowds dead.

Yeah.

He wont of made it.

Cant know for show.

I do. You love him?

Dowd?

I love him. Like a bro. Not like I love you.

Aban show a burnin in his face an the sun aint to blame. It spread in a hot flood down his throat. Efia make like in the dark she dont see it, tho she too feel she glow like a coal.

Efia, say Aban. It aint right.

How so aint right? Whats past is like roots. Aint the whole tree if an you only know the trunk.

I cant put it into speaks. It just dont feel right.

That first night, say Efia, Dowd tell us how he come to be here. He give us his life like a story an it get so we could love him straightway. Cos we know where he come from. Cos he got roots an we see em. But I aint never seen you Aban.

It aint sound talkin like this. Its like crossin some line an I dont –

OK.

Dont ask me.

I dint mean nuthin.

We gotta go back. Find Davys Way.

If you reckon.

Find it an the others. Malk Rona Becca. Aban Efia. Back like it use to be.

Well you can try, say Efia an she push no more gainst him. Aban crawl out to set up dewcloths. She stay to fix some supper. Crush locusts to make flour. Wont try that again. Wont ask him questions. Wont mention neither the names he forget.

Two slow days an no trace of Davys Way. Only the burnin land an bust-up steds like the Roamin town of Silster. We smell it first, see its smoke risin an keep out its way. Haulin thirst like a rider on our backs. Till without meanin to we enter Pamper Heave, or whats left of it. Rusty skulls of oil lamps, old farmin tools, broke pots an pans. Grindin stones in the ash shadow of burnout huts. Dead camels an mules, like the bones an ribs of bust-up furniture.

Hoofers dint get much.

For show, say Efia. Not least cos they aint bin here.

We find a well behind a meetin tree. Aban pull hard at the bucket rope when a voice from the tree say, Forget it.

A woman sit gainst the tree, a bloke beside her starin at the ground. Efia see the wrong angle of his hand, like its broke.

Whats up with the well?

Whats down it you mean. Dead girl. Been there two days. Cant you smell her?

Aban look at the dumb bloke. Whats wrong with his hand?

He kill a man with it. Cant use it now for three days. Wash off the polushun.

Aban go to the well, lean over it then push back gaggin.

Told you, say the woman.

Hoofers?

Thats how they want it to look. Blame yer foes. Take care no one live to say otherways.

All this for what? Land?

Why you ask girl? Men kill men an land remain. Lands there for itself an dont ask blokes to fight for it. So they say the Law wannit or bosses in the Wen. But thats just talk. War *need* talkin up cos no one ud do it otherways.

Efia look to a deep gash in the womans leg. The woman cover it with a bloody hand. Efia look her in the eye. This hard person. Like she might find kindness there.

Is now worse an ever? Howd we get so bad?

Things badder thats all. Times harder an no rains whip up more an dust.

But alls so *ugly*, say Efia an her voice break.

Wars ugly, say the woman, its face aint changin. It smell an it taste like its done before the Fast Time.

You got water, say Aban.

Nope.

Need some?

Cant give you nuthin for it.

How bout directions?

Tho we dont have much in our jercans, Efia watch Aban fill a cap an bring it to the woman. She take a sip then look at her bloke.

Got some for him too?

OK.

Aban refill the cap an the woman lift it to the blokes lips. He drink, tho its like hes sleepin with his eyes open.

Aint got more?

Need it for us, say Aban, takin back the cap. The woman nod an her eyelids droop. She open em again like she just recall we there. Where you headin, she say.

West.

Try Oldermaster. Reckon theres folk still there. Go careful tho. Oldermasters where Davy use to live. More for a drop eh?

Efia take the jercan from Abans grip. Wait, he say, but she hand it to the woman who look for a sec at Aban before takin a gulp. Ta girl. Ta for that.

There aint no Davy, say Aban.

Look around you.

Thats men.

Ole Davy win men over do his work for him. He give us fire you know that? Na. Alls forgot innit. Cept you know now. The truth walk in you. Well Davys got plans for us he give us fire an lots of nifty stuff. Give men all they big thinks in the Fast Time an Oldermasters where they make em happen. Yer spear my blokes axe they aint *straws* to what they forge at Oldermaster. Back in the good ole then what give us the bad ole now.

If its so bad, say Aban, why go there?

Cos its big enuf I reckon folk aint all fled an you get supplies. If an you got, say the woman, grinnin, what stedders want to buy.

Aban see her eyes run over Efias body. Lets go, he say.

Efia catch him up. Oldermasters risky –

Better an listen to that old witch.

I hear you, the woman say but she dont seem to care, shes munchin her gums, lookin at her bloke. His eyes shut now an she pluck a thread of spit off his chin.

Will you be OK, say Efia.

No, say the woman, dont expect so. But nuthin you can do bout it.

She tell us how to cross country to Oldermaster an Efia speak her thanks. Tho once we set off, an Pamper Heaves smoulderin behind us, its a lightness she feel in her body.

We camp at dusk in sight of Davys manshuns.

—————

Good enuf place for sleepin, say Aban.

Efia smile cos its way better. Too small for a waterin place, still its green in the grey, a sign of life. Aban dig down to mucky water an Efia find funnel an fat hen that keep the gumdrip away. Aban havin strong teeth chew the funnel stalk an bulb. Efia mash up fathead an grubs she dig up before Silster.

Look cross the waste to Oldermasters ramparts. No lights behind, nor folk to see gainst the evenin sky.

All gone you reckon?

Dunno, say Aban. Not so we can risk a fire.

Strain ditch water thru muslin strips an drink it. Eat next an Efia think out loud on her past when she use to be sure of one meal a day. Water too in the winter months from chalk streams. She tell Aban how her pa bring back from market sacks of beans, a can of cookin oil, salt an flour. Now its only foragin an shoppin. An not much of the second since Winsham an we lose Lan.

Cross the hills the sun melt into sand an its evenin. Birds group in the trees over us. Warbles with they scritchy yek an sad bush robins. A flock of budjis clingin to branches chat an clamber with they beaks. Off in the scrub a goat-sucker start its purrin. Aban lay a hand on Efias foot. You ask me, he say, to talk some. Bout me. Bout what its like to be Aban.

Yeah.

Stuff we dont give. When we group. Stuff we carry on our lonesum.

Tell me.

How?

Where you feel it.

He sit in the shadow of him. Slow thru speakin he come out from it. He tell Efia bout his folks in Whey Bitch. How poor his pa, how sick his ma with eight kids an Aban the youngest. No cash for drugs nor medics, he watch his brother Tom die. Sumthin in his gut burst. Nuthin they can do. When Malair carry off his pa his uncle Silas take him to the Wen. Tell him its to buy skins but its Aban his uncles meanin to sell. To Feo for a life of labour. Meet Malk that first night in they Hamsted cell. Malk who tell him, You a slave boy now an no mistake. Feo got yer for long as he fancy an there aint no scapin it till Death fancy you more. But Malk dont mean bad, dont treat him hard after sayin that. He take him on, show him the ropes. Malk an Aban get to be like bros. Workin for Feo.

Not so hard at first, say Aban. But Feo start drinkin an he get bad. Real filthy. It get so we cant take no more. I steal his knife. We do Feo in bed an run away. Scape slaves an killers you know why we fraid of arrest.

Who done the killin?

Eh?

Who cut Feos throat?

Aban look out cross the waste an toss bits of twig at it. Efia, he say, I wish we aint come to this. You an me. I wish we stay like before the Winsham raid. Before Dowd come an we lose Lan an everythin.

Its dark now in the copse an Efia speak close to his ear. Nuthin stay like it is, she say, nor you want it. Nor nuthin stay like you dont. Its just the way of it Aban. Make you hut an joy the roof but dont call it home cos there aint no home for us in this world only passin places. Only thirsty road an everythin changin.

Aban look at Efia. He hold her with his eyes till she cant move. She dont see his thinks but she can feel em, like a dark animal sittin between us. Then he reach inside his pack an take out the stone he bin carvin.

For you, he say.

Efia feel him put the stone in her hand. Its damp from his skin, like the stones made of flesh. Abans sweat on it like dew. Efia try to give it back but he fold her fingers over it till she feel its hips, the necklace round its throat an breast.

Its her, she say.

She give it to me. She tell me what to do. Like she guide my fingers.

Efia take it then. Hold it to her heart. Put her lips to the grooves an speak holy things. Say Lans name. Say Dowds. Take em into yer body. Take em home Momma. Back to the ground where everythin finish an everythin start.

Aban listen to her pray. The Laws losin its grip on him. Whats left of the Law in a world the Law made.

Maybe he see Momma too.

*

I lower the stone. Lay her gentle in my lap.

Aban kiss me on the mouth an I feel my body quake. Like hes the sun an Im the land gone all shimmery under him. I reach out but he move away. I cant say nuthin to call him back. Not cos I dont want to but cos I want it too much.

Later, I dont know when. Later I wake up. It grab me from sleep like a cat snatch a mouse. Take me in its jaws an squeeze till Im sobbin from the pain. My heart burnin,

my lungs wont take no air, all I can think is Lans laugh an
her terror dance, Dowds fight with the bush an the crack
of juntamens guns. How the smell of corses stain yer
thinks an once its in yer head you wont never wash it out.

Hey, say Aban touchin me. He reach for the stone he
give me an press it in my hand. He kiss the wet an sand
from my cheeks. I feel the rough on his chin. Taste salt on
his lips an tongue. Skin an sand an the woods close over
us, like the worlds foldin its wings in a whisper of leaves.
No group left but only him an me. The world all before us.
A short sleep away.

Aban wake first an look fraid for the group but find only
me. Efia. Pressin gainst him in the cool. He slap his cheek
to think him into the here an whats just bin. Our trek to
Oldermaster, whats spoke between us, the bloke with
polushun on his hands. Aban lift him on his elbows an
look out cross the warmin-up scrub. Oldermaster look
empty. Worth the risk? An survivors ready to kill for what
remain of grub an water? Go round is better. Leave Davys
sted to Davy an his mates.

I sit up with a warnin like a shout in my head. Aban say,
Watcher but I shush him quick.

What?

Listen.

Abans upright, every nerve prickin. He pat the ground
for his pack an sharpstick. He look at me, searchin for my
thinks. I dont hear nuthin, he say.

There.

Like the moon sometime show up in the mornin sky, a
sound creep out from the heave noises. Bird chatter, carder
song, the rasp of fronds an sand an there in em all, but

comin closer, the sound of footfalls. Aban think at once its danger but in the shuffle a tiny sound, a tingle in the ear, the ring of a bell. Not like cattle clonk or gungalung of goat bells but a thin white mutter, like a flower quiverin in the breeze.

Aban *where you goin*, I say cos hes creepin thru weeds away from me.

Stay there, he whisper an I do like he say tho footsteps an the bell grow louder till Im fraid an quakin. Sod this, I reckon an press on my hands an toes to the copses edge.

On the track I see folk comin. Movin slow like they drunk an tryin not to look it. Six grownups, tho whether blokes or women who can say cos they all wrap up in grey jelabas. Six grownups an four kiddies between em. At first I think *slavers* cos it look like the kiddies are tie to a rope. A length of rope tight an the walkers movin not like they carryin it but like its movin em. The bell speak louder an I see it on the front childs neck an all a sudden I get it. These kids aint captive, they steerin the others. Lookin forward an side to side whiles the grownups in they jelabas seem to sniff the air, they heads wanderin an I look for they eyes, see the lids red an raw, the skin gone thick like elbow scurf. Feel a cold pain in my chest, like deep thirst, like the pain I feel when Lan get took in Winsham. Crouchin low I watch the blind folk an they escorts. Into my head quick thinks, like where they come from, where they headin an how in all the dangers of drought an fightin do they get there safe? Six riverblind grownups an they small seein guides.

While I chew on these thinks a cry not of crit or bird fly out from the trees.

Aban?

The cry again, like foxy at night, an the kiddies stare, the blind folk snuffle an grope. A stick fly quiverin into the track, it bury its head only yards from the blind folk an all on a sudden the trees shred, yelpin bodies rushin feathery with leaves an sharpsticks. Too late the guides pull on the rope to speed the grownups but they panic, one on em run into furze an fall bleatin, two more drop to they knees, hands together like they prayin to the Law, tho I know the Law aint in the savin bizness. In a few leaps more the attackers gonna reach em. From the head-dress of one I see a flame of red hair. The name scape my lips before I can catch it back an Im out of the copse runnin an Abans beside me runnin too an the breath tearin out of us.

Malks got the guidin stick up like hes gonna bring it down on a blind mans skull when Aban throw him at his legs. The boys churn the dust where they tumble an Nathins racin at em, his sharpstick ready. Becca stare from the boys to me whos callin her name like a ghost come from the grave.

Stop! Becca stop him!

Malk kick Aban off his legs. He sit on his arse starin. Then turn to Nathin say, Round em up, cos the blind groups back together an gettin away. Nathin do like hes told, jerkin his spear an yippin.

Aban lurchin for breath find no room to speak.

You gonna help us? Malk look at Aban an me. The leaves torn an broke off his face, we see dirt an a wound like a slug of dry blood on his cheek. Well?

Help you, I say, do what?

Fucks sake. We reckon we *lost* you.

Tell us you aint plannin on robbin these folk.

Malk gob into his hand. Shit Aban you cut my knee. Aban say nuthin, he just watch his bro spitwash his wound. Dont spose you find Dowd on yer way?

Wheres Rona, say Aban.

Shes safe, say Malk. Near Pamper Heave. Leave her there with a bust ankle. So you see, he turn to me, why we aint got time to nabber. Stedders got grub in they packs now help us take it off em.

No, say Aban.

What?

I cant let you.

Malk act like he dont hear this, he nod an pick sand out his cut. He lean on the guidin stick then look squintin at Nathin an Becca who got the blind folk an the kiddies kneelin on the ground. Easy for you, say Malk to Aban. You aint got no group to lead. Who else gonna feed us? You? Malks eyes set on me an a grin show in his dirty face. Then he swing the guidin stick like a club on his shoulder an make for the captives. Only Aban run an block his way.

Now Aban …

Dont.

Malk sniff, calm enuf, only a nerves twitchin in his neck. All I can do is watch an from where blind folk kneelin Nathin Becca do likeways. Malk lower the guidin stick. He turn it over in his hands like hes lookin at the grain of its wood, then press its head in Abans chest. Aban push it away. Slow an easy Malk do it again. Aban grab the head of the stick an Malk put his weight behind it. Only Aban step aside an his own strength land Malk in the dust. Aban put out a hand for him. But Malk dont take it, he make a fist of sand an toss it in Abans face.

Aban cry out an Malk dive hard into his belly. Aban stagger back an fall an now the boys are rollin on the ground. Its like each is tryin to hug the fight out of the other. No speaks come from em, no sound almost, only they breaths an the stony scrabble of they bodies. Nathin walk over, his sharpstick ready but Becca grab him by the ankle. He try to kick free of her till she catch him with the look on her face an he stop tryin. Becca meet eyes with me cross the sand. Her face too all cut an dirty. Her sorrow just like mine. We watch Malk writhe under Aban, reachin for the guidin stick where it fall. But Abans that bit stronger or more clever, he catch Malks arm an pin it back till Malk scream in pain.

Get off him, shout Becca.

Abans in control now. I watch him tight his hold on Malk. Grapple up to grip him with his legs. Each twist an squirm makin it worse, till Malk go limp. Aban his slaver for a sec. Rider of a broken beast. An like Im lookin straight into Abans thinks I see him hate this. He look at the back of Malks head. At the head of his bro. It look small to him, the hair like feathers, oily with sweat. An Aban loose his grip on Malk. Loose it an start to get off him.

Only Malk dont stay down. His leg jerk up an catch Aban in the balls. Aban stagger an Malks on him, his fist risin an fallin, risin an fallin, like a man doin heavy work. Each blow a dull thud. Im screamin for this to stop, I got my spear up, Nathin lift his own to fling at me an in Malks fist theres a big flint. He hold it high over Abans face. Ready to bring it down. The flints got a dull coat but I can see a sharp ridge on it. Malk lift the flint higher. Aban dont move, he just lie bloody an pantin. The boys look into each others cut an swellin eyes.

The flint come down. But not with Malks strength behind it. His fingers open an the stone drop safe on the sand.

Malk get wincin to his feet. I drop my spear an run for Aban where hes lyin.

Stay there, say Malk to Nathin case they give the blind folk a chance to get free. The hang of Malks face I seen before, after our groupin. Like hes all done. Its good you alive, say Malk to me. Come with us Efia.

Where?

You know where.

But Aban –

Malk shrug an suck at his pain. I reckon he follow where you go.

Yeah but we dont want him, say Nathin. Callin out from where he stand with Becca. He look over to where Abans in the dust. After what he done to us. You know its Aban set the trapper loose. Undone his bonds an his boys.

No, I say.

He show the guidin stick no respect. Let our foes run away from us. Aban aint trusty.

That were me, I say. *I* set the heave bloke free. He were no enemy to us an you know it Malk. We had no call to tie em up.

Nathin shout at me for it, Bitch!

I let em go.

Well, say Malk after deep breaths. Leastways you tell us.

An I aint comin with you now.

Becca moan at this. Efia we need you. Rona an me.

I cant.

What, say Malk. You reckon you do elseways?

Dunno. Maybe help em, an I nod at the blind captives. What they got you can take Malk? Howd it help to rob em?

Food.

But they cant *see*. You can still look for life but they?

Malk gaze from me to the folk. Nathin snag his eye an say, Malk no! They fair game. We gotta do it.

Where you take em then?

Wherever they goin. With kiddies how they gonna stay safe? Maybe with us they get there.

Us?

Me an Aban.

I see pain once more tho not of flesh in Malks face. He look slow like he must but dont want to over his shoulder at Aban, whos sittin up now holdin his head. I want to cry at the mess of his face. But I keep it in me.

Efia, say Malk, goin lones a curse. Worse an bein ouster cos most ousters got folk but loners? They creep with no friend nor bro. In a group you share even whats smallest thats how you survive. The group share everythin it live like one. You an him go lonesum you be corses before the years out.

Still thats what we doin. So if you wanna rob the blind you gotta rob us too. Here, I say an shrug the pack off my shoulder, swing it long my arm an hold it out to Malk. Take it.

Malk shake his head. Becca behind him say, Whats goin on? Whats she doin?

Take it if you want it. I cant stop you.

Keep yer pack, say Malk an the blood drain from whats showin of his face. Keep it an him an *they* if thats what you want. If deaths what you after. Then he hold up the guidin stick an walk towards the trees. Nathin Becca starin after.

Hey! What bout –?

Come on, say Becca to Nathin an shes runnin to catch up with Malk. Aban dont see her go. Nor Nathin up spear, kickin dust at a blind woman, then off into the scrub.

I walk to where Abans sittin an put a hand on his shoulder to steady me. Best clean you up, I say.

Malk –

Hes gone.

The group –

Its OK. Just you an me now.

I cant see.

Theres muck in yer eyes. Skin swoll up is all.

Tippin water from my jercan, I dab his face with my hem. Whiles I wash away the blood an Aban moan, his fingers on my wrists, I hear footfalls behind us. The scuffin of blind folks feet. The surer steps of seein kids. Without turnin I can feel the tug of they questions. The weight of they need. The bell sleepin on the small boys chest. Askin the world for mercy. The guidin rope slack between em as they gather. Turnin to us cos there aint no one else. Waitin for two who can lead em into nightfall.

The sun was fierce. It blazed, a great warrior, on the heath and raised a sweat on the brows of three children gone, against instruction, to spy on the great doing beyond their world.

His cousin was happy to hold his hand and he hers, for none of his friends was present to call him a baby. Their palms were hot and tacky with blackberry juice. His brother swung a switch through the blossoming heather.

They walked far from the prying eyes of home.

'Here it is,' his brother said, and turned to reveal a ghoulish expression.

His cousin laughed. It was a great dare, and he would not be frightened though he was the smallest, and he did not mind their teasing, for it meant they kept him close and let him come along.

A gash had been made in the world. He was afraid to look at it and at the men labouring in it like maggots in a wound. The wound ran deeper into the world than he had ever travelled. He could hear no birdsong above the clang-our of stone.

There were soldiers leaning on their shields, gazing dully into the heath. They stared at the nearest, a stocky man with hairy forearms and a plump neck.

It was hard to fathom this being – its physical weight in the world.

He contemplated the point of the javelin and followed the shaft till he saw the hand that gripped it and the thumb which was barely a stump. He dragged on his brother's wrist to share with him what he saw but his brother snatched back his arm and the movement, or else the pressure of their attention, made the soldier turn his head.

Children and soldier exchanged stares. Under his helmet, the soldier's soul was unreachable.

The soldier nudged his neighbour, and now two soldiers were watching him and his brother and cousin, who had only come to see this work that everyone whispered about and feared and marvelled at.

The second soldier spoke. It was a strange language and his words dropped like a piece of gristle thrown to a dog. None of the children knew what to do or say in reply.

The soldier tossed a second word-bone at them and his neighbour sniggered. His cousin was tugging at them to retreat but his brother would not. His brother took a step towards the soldiers and they growled at him.

His brother took another step. The fat soldier made a monstrous face and *roared* –

– and they were running now, away from the road and the laughing soldiers. Part of him knew this was pretend fear, but it was difficult to tell for sure and he ran the fastest, his fright chasing him until he was far from everyone, the soldiers and his brother and cousin.

A heaviness came into his legs and slowed him till he was alone with his heart and his racing breath and the knowledge that he was lost.

He knew, from his father, to ignore the voice that would lead him further into difficulty. He looked at his surroundings, trying to make sense of the place, not daring to call out lest he summon bad spirits.

He walked into the shade of a very tall beech. He touched the wounds in its bark and heard woodlarks behind him and stonechats. A green woodpecker flashed from a tussock of grass where it had been licking for ants. He went to the tussock, for ants intrigued him with their busy comings and goings.

It was there, in a scrape of exposed turf, that he found the stone. The other flints were mute but this one spoke. He picked it up and stared at it, turning the carvings in his hand and mind. It was by no means beautiful, but how snugly it fitted the width of his palm, its shape almost human though lacking arms or legs. He sat in the whispering grass and stroked the lines, like rings in wood but on the outside. He forgot about his fear. A companionable sweat pooled in the small of his back. He gave himself up to daydream, until he looked up from the stone and recognised the place.

He had been here before, laying traps with his grandfather. The beech tree shimmered in the heat. Butterflies flopped among its branches. He held the stone, or the stone held him. It was a gift that would guide him home: a mystery for him to hold and keep safe.

There was a great sigh, like the rushing of waters, above his head. He looked into the shaken curtain of leaves.

The beech was ancient, its trunk scarred and wrinkled like the hide of a beast. Andagin turned to watch it contend with the wind, and his spirit soared into the green boughs and the stone rolled over in his palm. He was a bird, high in that shifting canopy. He thought: the trees have no soul but the wind, and the wind has no body but the trees. And what being would he have – he, son of Brennos and Vala, youngest of the hill-fort clan – without this love that called him home?

Acknowledgements

The author wishes to thank Creative Scotland for financial assistance in the writing of this novel.